# THE RED LOTTERY TICKET

Owing to the antiquity and rarity of this book, certain pages are regrettably absent, and readability is compromised due to the blurring of the original text. If you possess any insights regarding the availability of these missing sections, kindly inform us. Your assistance is crucial in ensuring the completion of this significant work for the benefit of future generations.

# THE RED LOTTERY TICKET.

BY FORTUNE DU BOISGOBEY.

GYAN

*Published by*

Gyan Publishing House
5, Ansari Road
Daryaganj, New Delhi-110002
Phone: 011-47034999, 9811692060
E-mail: books@gyanbooks.com

*Distribution Network*
gyanbooks.com
India, USA, Canada, UK, Australia



ISBN: 978-93-6208-366-1 (HB)
First Published, 1887

2nd Impression 2024

*Printed at:* Gyan Press, Delhi.



**THE RED LOTTERY TICKET**
Author: FORTUNE DU BOISGOBEY

# THE RED LOTTERY TICKET.

# THE RED LOTTERY TICKET.

By FORTUNE DU BOISGOBEY.

# THE RED LOTTERY TICKET.

## I.

One day early in April, the month when the lilacs flower and when women begin to display light apparel, a cab could be seen crossing the bridge which spans the Seine between the Faubourg St. Germain and the Louvre, and which is known to the Parisians as the Pont des Saints Pères. The vehicle was going at a quiet trot, and it was driven by a jovial jehu, who hummed a song as he cracked his whip and jerked his reins. Both windows were down, and from each of them came a cloud of bluish smoke—the smoke of the cigars of two young fellows who were gaily chatting inside, and who, although they came from the so-called "Latin Quarter" of Paris, were quite unlike the students immortalised by Gavarni's pencil. They were, indeed, dressed with careful taste, and displayed none of the questionable manners which may be acquired in the drinking dens of the Boulevard St. Michel. One of them, a fair-haired young fellow with soft blue eyes, was named George Caumont, and was the son of a Norman cattle breeder, who lived on his land, saving up his cash, and making his only child an allowance of three thousand francs a year, so that he might complete, in Paris, the study of law which he had commenced at Caen. The other, a dark young man with curly moustaches and a bold expression of face, was the son of a petty nobleman of Périgord, who had left him a heavily mortgaged estate with a somewhat high-sounding name. He was called Adhémar de Puymirol, and lived upon a small allowance made him by an aunt who wished him to become a doctor.

He and George Caumont had met shortly after their arrival in Paris, and their acquaintance had speedily become intimacy, for they had the same ambition and much the same tastes. They both regarded their present situation as a probationary one, hoping sooner or later to contract a brilliant marriage; and they governed themselves accordingly, merely attending the courts and the clinical lectures when they had nothing better to do, and just occasionally passing an examination in order not to discourage Papa Caumont and Aunt Bessèges. But everything comes to an end, and with their relatives grumbling and their creditors barking loudly, there were days when the thought of the future filled them with dismay. Still, on this beautiful spring morning, everything seemed tinged with a roseate hue, and they even laughed at the enforced departure for the provinces apparently so near at hand. "Leave Paris!" said Adhémar, gazing at the scene around him. "Never, George; I would rather give lessons in anatomy to freshmen than go and bury myself in Périgord to doctor my aunt's farmers."

"And I," sighed George, "would rather act as a college tutor than devote the rest of my life to cattle breeding. We are at the end of our tether, unfortunately, and if we don't meet two rich girls before the close of the term, we shall be obliged to decamp, for Paris will be too hot for us."

"Ah, well, we will go to one of the watering-places where heiresses are met."

"You are always so confident!"

"That is the only way to succeed. If our friend Pierre Dargental had become discouraged, we shouldn't now be going to celebrate the close of his bachelor life at lunch. Dargental is no better than we are, and yet he has found a widow of title worth more than a million francs."

"And all he brings her on his side will be his debts—some three hundred thousand francs."

"Oh! in this part of the world, a man shrewd enough to obtain credit to that amount can aspire to anything—"

"Except to the hand of an honest woman," replied George. "There are some pretty hard stories about this Countess de Lescombat's behaviour after her first husband's death."

"Well, they say she accepted Dargental's offer of marriage before her period of mourning expired. She consoled herself a little too soon, perhaps, but that is a matter of no consequence, after all."

"All the same, I should much prefer a less wealthy and more innocent girl to a rich lady of rank, with a very doubtful reputation."

"But one can't always have one's choice in such matters. Dargental is about to enter a very wealthy set. He will introduce us to it, and we ought to succeed in finding what we want there. So it does not become us to find fault with him."

"Will any of his old flames be at lunch to-day?" inquired George.

"I believe that Blanche Pornic, the actress, is the only favoured one."

"She is very amusing."

"Yes; and thoroughly good-hearted."

The vehicle had crossed over the Place du Carrousel, and was now behind five or six others, which had formed into a line to pass through the narrow passage conducting into the Rue de Rivoli. "Five minutes to twelve!" exclaimed Puymirol, glancing at his watch. "They will be at table by the time we reach the Lion d'Or. Why doesn't this idiot of a cabman drive faster?"

"It isn't his fault. The block prevents him from doing so. There are at least half a dozen traps ahead of us."

As George spoke, he put his head out of the window, and saw that the passage would not be free for several minutes. Three or four pedestrians, tired of waiting, had turned to retrace their steps; and among them Caumont noticed a man wearing a broad-brimmed hat, pulled down over his eyes, and a full black beard concealing the lower part of his face. At a distance of ten paces behind him came two unprepossessing individuals, who seemed anxious not to lose sight of this bearded individual. Caumont rather lightly concluded that they were detectives watching the fellow, but as he had no personal interest in the matter he again ensconced himself in his corner and said to his friend: "Have a little patience. We shall soon move on." As he spoke, he turned, and failed to see that the bearded man rested his hand for an instant on the door of the vehicle, and then without glancing at the occupants, dropped something that fell upon Puymirol's boot.

"What is that?" cried Adhémar, "what scoundrel ventures to bombard us in this style?"

"I have no idea," replied George, and on hastily turning again, he caught a fresh glimpse of the bearded man, whose back only was now visible, for he had passed them, and was slowing proceeding across the Place du Carrousel. Just then the cab moved on, and in an instant the pedestrians were left far behind. "Whatever the article is it must have been thrown in by a man who just passed us," resumed George; "and he must have done so with extraordinary swiftness and dexterity, for his movement escaped my notice entirely."

Meanwhile Puymirol had picked up from the bottom of the cab a handsome pocket-book, which, with his friend's assent, he now began to open. "The man who threw that in here," said George, "must be a thief, who in his anxiety to escape arrest, and to get rid of the stolen article, dropped it into our cab. When pickpockets find themselves in danger of capture, they very often resort to that device."

"Well," rejoined Puymirol, "at least there isn't the slightest vestige of a bank-note inside, as you can see for yourself. Nor are there any visiting-cards, nothing but papers, and not many of them. In this compartment there are some lottery tickets, just look: The Tunisian Lottery, the Amiens Lottery, and the Lottery of the Decorative Art Society. And here on the other side there are some letters."

"Letters!" repeated George. "So much the better. We shall perhaps find in them some clue that will enable us to discover the person from whom the pocket-book was stolen."

"You don't know whether it was stolen," remarked Adhémar. "Besides, who would think of stealing lottery tickets?"

"True, but it perhaps contained money, which the thief extracted before throwing away; besides, a letter is sometimes of great value to its writer."

"Hum, these ones were written by women. There are three of them—each in a different handwriting, and, strange to say, not one of them signed, not even with a Christian name. The owner of the pocket-book must have had uncommonly prudent sweethearts. I wonder why he kept these notes in this case?"

"Because he intended to make use of them at some future time."

"You think he was a blackmailer, eh? That's quite possible."

"That theory would at least explain the robbery. If the women in question knew that these specimens of their handwriting had fallen into our hands, they would be more easy in mind, for we don't know them, and it is not likely that we ever shall."

"We are not sure of that. Stranger things than that happen in Paris. But do you think it advisable for us to take the pocket-book to the lost property office at the Prefecture of Police?"

"No, I think it would be better to burn it with its contents."

"Why? I feel strongly inclined to preserve it. One never knows what may happen, and it would afford me infinite satisfaction to discover one of these unknown correspondents."

"Do so if you like, but I don't want to mix myself up in any such affair. I shall forget the matter, and I beg that you will never remind me of it."

"Agreed, on conditions that you say nothing about it to any one at lunch. There will be a parcel of chatterers present."

"You need have no fears of that. I will be as silent as a fish."

"All right, then. Here we are! I must put these letters out of sight," said Puymirol, and he stowed the Russian leather-case away in his coat pocket.

The cab had drawn up in front of the Lion d'Or restaurant in the Rue du Helder, and the two friends alighted, and asked for the room reserved for M. Dargental's party. The head-waiter replied that the gentleman referred to had not yet arrived, though he had ordered lunch to be served at twelve o'clock precisely; and he then led the friends to an apartment where they found two people waiting. One of them was a pale young man, about twenty-eight years of age, as phlegmatic as a Scandinavian, and as dissipated as a Russian. Although always ready to drink, to play cards, and to spend his nights in bad company, he never laughed and rarely smiled. A good-hearted fellow, however, and popular in the set he mingled with. His name was Charles Balmer, and he was afflicted with the belief that he was dying from consumption. Beside him in the private room sat Blanche Pornic, the actress, Dargental's old flame. Tall, and lithe of form to a degree that had won her the surname of the Reed, she was very charming, with her pale golden hair, her brown eyes, sparkling with mischief, her regular features, her graceful movements, and her silvery voice—a voice that went straight to one's heart. When Puymirol and Caumont arrived she and Balmer were complaining of Dargental's non-arrival, and after some comments had been exchanged concerning his delay, Blanche exclaimed:

"We have given him quite enough grace. Come, Balmer, ring, and tell them to serve us."

"Nothing would please me better," exclaimed Balmer. "I am as hungry as a dog."

"That is a good sign for a sick man," remarked Puymirol.

"By no means. What, can it be that you, a medical man, are ignorant of the fact that consumptives eat like ogres?"

"That is all bosh; besides, you are no more a consumptive than I am."

"I haven't more than two years to live, as I know perfectly well. If you wish to satisfy yourself on the point, you only have to examine my lungs."

"No, no," cried Blanche. "This is no hospital, and you disgust me with your medical talk. To table, gentlemen! I will sit opposite Dargental. He isn't here, but I will imagine that he is. Caumont may take a seat on my right, and Puymirol on my left. And now let us partake of the funereal repast."

"Funereal is the very word," said Adhémar. "The invitations we received had mourning borders."

"And the bill of fare also," chimed in George.

"Pierre made a great mistake," remarked Blanche; "such jokes always bring bad luck."

"The fact that he hasn't come is sufficient proof of that. I wonder if he has broken a leg."

"No, indeed! Dargental is too lucky to meet with any such accident. His noble betrothed must have got wind of this breakfast, and have forbidden him to attend it."

"In that case, he would, at least, have warned you."

"Do you regret his absence?" asked Blanche, with a glance at Puymirol.

"How can I when I am near you?"

"Nonsense! you always will be a provincial. Confine your attention to these oysters. They are delicious, and this Sauterne is of the best quality."

This preliminary chat was soon interrupted by the lively clatter of knives and forks, and the tinkling of glasses. All the gentlemen of the party ate and drank heartily, but Blanche, despite her commendatory words, did not seem inclined to finish her oysters, and only just moistened her lips in the Château Yquem. "What is the matter with you, Blanche?" cried Balmer, between two mouthfuls. "I have seen you eat with a much better appetite. Is Pierre's marriage the cause of this falling off? You must have been expecting it for several months, however."

"I was so well prepared for it that I myself urged him to take the step. And as for being angry, that can hardly be, as I came expressly to lunch with him. He no longer cares for me; well, no matter, I can only rely on his wife to avenge me. She has already given conclusive proofs of her ability in that direction."

"Indeed?" inquired Balmer, with an air of pretended innocence.

"If you don't know her story, I will tell it you," rejoined Blanche abruptly.

"I know only what Dargental has seen fit to tell us," said Balmer.

"Well then, once upon a time, as they sat in fairy tales, there lived in Lyons a silk-worker, who had an illegitimate daughter. She was very beautiful, but she was no better than her mother. Her father vainly tried to repress her evil tendency, but at the age of fifteen, tired of being whipped and scolded, she eloped with a mountebank, under whose tuition she learned a host of things—circus-riding, trapeze-performing, and so forth."

"All the elegant accomplishments!" sneered Balmer.

"Two years afterwards, Octavia Crochard, as she was called, appeared in a new character. A respectable old gentleman who had fallen in love with her sent her to a boarding school at Saint Mandé, where she passed as his niece, every one being ignorant of her antecedents. She was so clever naturally that she soon made up for lost time, and speedily became a very accomplished young woman. She even learned how to conceal her proclivities, but she was none the better for that. Not long afterwards the old gentleman died, leaving her, in his will, an income of twelve thousand francs, on conditions that she took his name."

"A nice condition! What an idiot he must have been!"

"Octavia was shrewd enough to behave herself after she left the boarding-school. She engaged a companion or chaperon, and, thanks to the recommendation of the lady-principal of the school which she had just left, she succeeded in securing an acquaintance with people of position, and before many months had elapsed, she made a conquest of another old simpleton, a *blasé* millionaire, who married her shortly afterwards."

"This is a very interesting story," said Balmer, as he emptied his fifth glass of champagne; "but what has it to do with the countess?"

"What! haven't you guessed that this same Crochard girl is now known as the Countess de Lescombat, and will soon take the name of Madame d'Argental?—Dargental with an apostrophe, be it understood, for she has insisted that Pierre should make this change in his name. In fact, to please her, he has purchased the title of marquis somewhere in Italy. Octavia does not wish to marry beneath her station."

"Have you communicated all this information to your friend Dargental?"

"No, I have taken good care not to do that. He would imagine I had invented the story, and slandered the countess, from jealousy. But he will hear it from plenty of others, by and by. He already knows that Lescombat bequeathed his entire fortune to his wife only about a month before his death, and he will learn, sooner or later on, that the pretended attack of apoplexy that killed the count was a plain case of suicide. The old nobleman felt so much regret at having despoiled his natural heirs that he poisoned himself with prussic acid."

"But why didn't he alter his will?" inquired George Caumont.

"He couldn't; Octavia watched him too closely. Besides, she is a perfect Circe, in her power to bewitch men. She has poor Dargental completely under her control, for it is evident she has confiscated him this morning."

Adhémar and George could not repress a smile. They plainly realised that Blanche would never forgive Dargental for deserting her. As for the story about Madame de Lescombat, they thought it advisable to believe merely half of it; but even that was quite enough to make them pity the imprudent man who was about to place himself at the mercy of this wily widow. However, after all, why should she want to marry him, as he was not worth a copper?

"Are you sure that he is at her house now?" inquired Balmer. "Remember, he may be ill."

"He lives but a short distance from here, on the Boulevard Haussmann. We might send a messenger there to inquire after him," suggested George.

"I object to that proposal," said Blanche. "He would imagine that I could not get on without him. Balmer, fill my glass. Gentlemen, I drink to your sweethearts."

The toast met with no response, for, at that moment, a waiter entered, bearing a salver upon which a blue envelope was lying. "Here is a telegram which has just arrived for Monsieur Dargental," said the attendant. "Shall I lay it beside his plate?"

"Hand it here!" cried Balmer, seizing hold of the missive. "A telegram is not a letter, and it will certainly do no harm for me to open this one. It will perhaps explain why Pierre has left us in the lurch, after inviting us here." He tore open the envelope as he spoke, and he had scarcely glanced at the contents, than he exclaimed triumphantly: "It is from the countess? You see that he is not at her house."

"Let me see it," said Blanche, holding out her hand; and, glancing at the missive, she added: "It is from her. Listen, gentlemen: 'My dear Pierre—I should be very sorry to curtail your farewells to your friends of both sexes, but I should be greatly obliged to you if you would come to my house immediately after the lunch.' Both sexes! that is a dig at me. This countess has a very easy style, and she is as prudent as a serpent, for she has merely signed her christian name, Octavia, for fear of compromising herself, I suppose."

As the actress spoke, she passed the telegram to her left-hand neighbour. Puymirol, on examining it, at once perceived that it was not a genuine telegram, but one of those communications, the sender of which pens as many words as he pleases upon a slip of paper; he then seals the latter up, and it is despatched by the pneumatic tube service to any part of Paris. The handwriting of this particular "telegraphic-note" was therefore the countess's, not a clerk's, and Adhémar noted that it was peculiarly firm and decided in character.

"Well," said Blanche, "as the countess hasn't kept Pierre a prisoner, I begin to think that he must be playing a trick on us."

"Unless some misfortune has befallen him," suggested Puymirol.

"A misfortune will befall him when he marries, there is no doubt of that; but Dargental has no business to treat us like nobodies. If you take my advice, we will each pay a share of the bill and decamp."

"Speak for yourself, I am still thirsty," growled Balmer. "You can go if you like, but I intend to have my coffee and season it with a few glasses of cognac."

"Then you can settle the bill, and I will send you my share of it as soon as I learn the amount. I am going. Who loves me, follows me!" said Blanche, rising from table.

Adhémar and George followed her example. "I shall pass Dargental's door on leaving here, and I will hand his doorkeeper that pneumatic telegram," remarked Adhémar, placing the missive in his pocket beside the pocket-book thrown into the cab.

Balmer declining to move, the three others now went downstairs together. Blanche then sprang into a cab which stood outside the restaurant and drove off, saying, "Come and see me one of these days. I should like to hear the end of this affair."

"What do you think of it all?" said Caumont to Adhémar, as soon as the actress had gone.

"I think," replied Puymirol, "that the countess is an adventuress, Blanche a viper, and Dargental a fool."

"Why, not long ago, you proclaimed him to be shrewdness personified!"

"I must confess that that opinion seems erroneous. But let us go to Dargental's place; we shall, perhaps, find the solution of the enigma there. It isn't far off."

The house in which Dargental lived stood on the Boulevard Haussmann. They soon reached the door, and the house-porter, on being questioned by Adhémar, replied that he believed that M. Dargental was at home. At all events, he had not seen him pass out. Dargental's rooms were situated on the second floor, to which the two friends duly climbed. Puymirol rang, but no one answered the summons, and the bell was pulled three times more, but without any better success. The two friends were, indeed, about to go off disappointed, when a servant in livery, carrying a package under his arm, appeared upon the landing. This servant was Dargental's valet, and he knew Puymirol and Caumont by sight. "I fear that the marquis has gone out," he remarked. On hearing this title, which Dargental had never borne before, the two friends exchanged a smile. "He was to lunch out to-day," continued the valet, "and he was already dressed when he sent me off on an errand at about eleven o'clock."

"It was with us that he meant to lunch, and we haven't seen anything of him," said Caumont.

"If you gentlemen would like to come in, I have the key," now suggested the servant.

"Very well, open the door, then."

The valet thereupon ushered them into an ante-chamber which they had traversed more than once. "Is there a fire in the house?" inquired Puymirol. "There is a strong smell of smoke here."

"Of powder, rather," muttered Caumont.

The valet, apparently quite as surprised by the smell as they were, opened the dining-room door, crossed the threshold, looked in, and then suddenly recoiled, exclaiming, in evident terror: "My God! my master is dead! Monsieur le marquis has killed himself!"

Puymirol pushed the valet aside, and rushed into the room. It was but dimly lighted by stained glass windows, and Puymirol did not at first perceive Dargental, upon whom the valet's eyes had chanced to fall just as he crossed the threshold. Madame de Lescombat's unfortunate lover was sitting, or rather reclining, in a large arm-chair. Seen from a distance, he seemed to be asleep. Puymirol hastened forward, took hold of his hand, found that it was icy cold, and then perceived that his face was livid, his eyes half closed, and his mouth distorted. "Open the window, quick, quick!" he cried, and Caumont, forestalling the valet, instantly obeyed the order.

In the full light it was seen that stains of blood tinged Dargental's shirt front, which was torn and scorched by a bullet in the vicinity of the heart; his waistcoat was unbuttoned, the lapels of his coat were pushed back and creased, while on the floor at his feet gleamed the shining barrel of a revolver. "My master! my poor master!" groaned the valet.

"You can not restore him to life, my lad," said Puymirol, who never lost his presence of mind. "This is no time for weeping. The commissary of police must be warned. Fetch him immediately, and, on your way out, tell the doorkeeper what has happened, and ask him to come up. We don't care to remain alone with the body. Upon the whole, it will be best for us to go down with you, I think. Our unfortunate friend is beyond all human aid, and the suicide must be established at once."

Neither Caumont nor the valet made any objections, and the trio hastened downstairs. "My master has shot himself," cried the valet to the doorkeeper. "These gentlemen can testify that I was not present when the accident occurred! On returning home, a few moments ago, I found them ringing at the door, so I opened it for them with my key."

"It is really impossible," said the doorkeeper in alarm. "I saw him this morning, and he seemed to be in the best of spirits. He even warned me that he meant to give up his apartments on account of his approaching marriage."

"We didn't come here to talk," interrupted Puymirol. "This fellow is going for the commissary of police; you had better come upstairs with us, and remain until he brings some official back with him."

The doorkeeper assented; the valet hastened off; and the two friends, having again ascended the stairs, this time with the cerberus of the house, re-entered the apartments where nothing had been disturbed during their absence. Not caring to approach the body, they all three of them remained in the ante-chamber. "Are you well acquainted with this valet?" Puymirol inquired of the doorkeeper.

"Yes, sir. He has been in Monsieur Dargental's employ for three years. I assure you that he is quite incapable of a crime, and fully deserves all the confidence my unfortunate tenant placed in him. This very morning, Monsieur Dargental gave him a letter for the Countess de Lescombat, his intended wife. I was standing at my door as he passed out, and Jean stopped for a moment to chat with me. While we were talking, he said: 'Ah! Monsieur Pinchon, I am so attached to my master that—'"

The sound of footsteps upon the stairs cut M. Pinchon short. The valet was returning, bringing with him in lieu of the commissary, who was absent from his office, that functionary's secretary, an intelligent, wide-awake-looking young man. Having been enlightened on the way by the servant, the secretary walked straight to the body, examined it carefully but without touching it, and said curtly: "This chair is not in its accustomed place."

The other chairs were, in fact, arranged in lines along the walls, but this one stood in the middle of the room, and almost directly opposite the door. "This is the first time I ever heard of a man sitting down to shoot himself," continued the official.

"Do you suspect a crime, then?" inquired Puymirol.

"I have formed no opinion as yet. A doctor will come with the commissary, and make a report. In the meantime, gentlemen, will you have the kindness to give me your names and addresses, for it does not seem necessary that you should be present at the investigation. You will be questioned later on, if needful."

"I am named Adhémar de Puymirol; my friend's name is George Caumont, and we live together, at No. 14, in the Rue de Medicis."

"Very well," said the secretary, as he entered the names in his note-book. "You were very intimate, I believe, with this Monsieur—"

"Monsieur Pierre Dargental," concluded Puymirol. "We certainly knew him very well; I especially. He had invited us to lunch with him this morning in company with Monsieur Charles Balmer, who resides, I believe, in the Rue Auber, and an actress named Blanche Pornic, who lives in the Avenue de Messine."

"Was the lunch ordered by Monsieur Dargental?"

"Yes, and we ate it without him. Afterwards we called here, my friend and myself, to ascertain what had become of him, and we were ringing at his door when the valet, who happened to come upstairs, opened it for us."

"I am aware of that. You must have been greatly surprised on entering. To what cause do you attribute this suicide?"

"I know no cause for it. Dargental was about to be married; besides, it seems to me very strange that he should have killed himself just as we were expecting him to celebrate the close of his bachelor life."

"Yes, and all the stranger as he was quite ready to go out. See, his hat has rolled behind the chair, and his cane has fallen upon the floor. All this does not seem to harmonize with the care he appears to have taken in seating himself."

"That is true. The whole affair is incomprehensible. Dargental must have momentarily lost his mind."

"In that case he must have had a revolver in his pocket at the time; but that weapon there is not one of the sort a man usually carries upon his person. It is too large and too heavy for that."

"All I can say is that the weapon belonged to him. I have often seen it hanging, with others, against the wall of his bedroom. I am certain that it must bear the name of the dealer who sold it to him—Galland."

"That point will be verified by the commissary, and the doctor will tell us if the blood could have spouted a distance of two yards from the arm-chair. See, here is a pool of it upon the floor, almost at my very feet." Puymirol hastily recoiled, for he perceived, for the first time, that he was almost stepping in it. "One more question, sir," said the 'secretary.' "Had Monsieur Dargental any enemies?"

"Not to my knowledge. On the contrary, he had many friends. Besides, no one could have anything to gain by his death, for he had no fortune."

"Oh, no," sighed the doorkeeper. "An execution was put in only the other day by one of his creditors."

"Nevertheless, he lived in handsome style," replied the secretary, "and it is very probable that he had more or less money in the house or about his person; in fact, judging from the apparent disorder of his clothing, it seems more than likely that his pockets were searched after his death. But I will detain you no longer, gentlemen. You will hold yourselves, of course, at the disposal of the authorities—I have your address."

"Certainly, sir," said Puymirol, who had had quite enough of this covert examination. George Caumont was also anxious to get away, for this talk in the presence of his friend's lifeless body made him sick at heart. The valet was about to beat a retreat with them, but the dismissal was not for him, for the secretary remarked drily: "Remain. The commissary will want to talk with you."

"I hope you have no further need of me," now said the doorkeeper.

"Yes, I have, but I shall not keep you long."

M. Pinchon's dismay was pitiful to behold, and the two friends hastily availed themselves of the permission to depart. "What do you think of this catastrophe?" inquired Puymirol, as soon as they reached the street.

"I really don't know what to think of it, and I must admit that I shall make no attempt to solve the mystery. The authorities will take charge of that."

"Well, Dargental did me many good turns, and I should like to avenge his death, for I really believe he was murdered."

"Indeed! But whom do you suspect? And what do you suppose was the object of the crime? Robbery?"

"No, he had nothing but debts. The porter, you recollect, told us that his furniture had been attached. Some woman committed the murder. A woman who was or who had been in love with him."

"Then she killed him from jealousy, you think?"

"Jealousy or revenge, which amounts to about the same thing. It must have been one of his recent flames, probably the last one."

"What, Blanche Pornic? But she lunched with us."

"It is just because she lunched with us that I suspect her. She came to the restaurant merely to prove an *alibi*. She may very well have killed Dargental at eleven o'clock and yet have reached the Lion d'Or before noon. Balmer can tell us at what hour she arrived. Besides, she may have hired some other person to commit the crime in her stead. By the way, have you forgotten what she said during lunch? Despite her sweet words one could guess that she hated Dargental."

"Indeed! why should she hate him?"

"Because he was going to marry Madame de Lescombat. She could not forgive him for preferring the countess to herself. And by the way, if the inquiry proves that Dargental has really been murdered, Blanche would be delighted should her rival be accused of the crime."

"Well, she certainly didn't act in the right way to divert suspicion from herself. It is strange that she should have treated us to that narrative of the countess's career quite unsolicited; and if she is as shrewd as you pretend—"

"Did you notice her strange manner during the repast, and her abrupt departure afterwards? She heard us say that we were going to Dargental's to find out what had become of him, and she did not care to await the result. She knew the cause of his absence only too well."

"You may call these indications, if you like," replied George, "still they hardly prove that Mademoiselle Pornic instigated the murder, and I don't think her capable of such baseness. Dargental must have committed suicide."

"Oh, a man doesn't kill himself like that with his hat on his head and a cane in his hand. It occurs to me now that his shirt was not scorched as much as it would have been if the pistol had been placed against it. The shot must have been fired from a distance of a few yards, and Dargental probably fell just where we saw the pool of blood. The murderer afterwards raised him up and seated him in the arm-chair."

"That's possible," muttered George, somewhat shaken in his convictions.

"Ah, you are coming round to my way of thinking, at last. Well, I return to my first injunction. Look for the woman. Where is the woman?"

"Well, if you feel so positive that a woman is mixed up in the affair," said Caumont, after a long pause, "I am surprised that you don't think of that countess whose first husband ended so badly."

"That's absurd!" exclaimed Puymirol. "The first husband committed suicide, and his widow certainly had no reason to make away with the man she meant to take as his successor."

"You know nothing about that."

"Mademoiselle Pornic's inuendoes will rankle in your mind, I see. You certainly place a deal of confidence in that venomous creature."

"I might retort that you seem to feel a great deal of confidence in the countess. Do you think of offering yourself as a substitute for Dargental?"

"No, but the countess is no worse than many other women, and your suspicions are too ridiculous to be entertained for a moment. Don't you recollect that telegram in which Madame de Lescombat said: 'I don't wish to interfere with your farewell entertainment to your friends of both sexes, but come and see me immediately afterwards.' So she must have known that Dargental was breakfasting with one or more of his old flames, and feeling no jealousy on that account, she had no grievance against him."

"Did she really say 'your friends of both sexes?'"

"Those were the very words, my dear fellow, as you shall see for yourself. I put the telegram in my pocket, you recollect, with the intention of giving it to Dargental. Here it is." And Adhémar, after rummaging in his pocket, drew from it not only the telegram, but also the mysterious pocket-book. Then, turning suddenly, he dragged George behind one of the newspaper kiosks on the boulevard, along which they were now walking. "Didn't Blanche say that Dargental had just been invested with the title of marquis?" he asked.

"Yes, and she must have told the truth, for the valet said, 'Monsieur le Marquis,' in speaking of his master."

"Blanche also said, did she not, that Dargental had altered his name to D'Argental?"

"To please the Countess de Lescombat. The news did not surprise me. For ennobling one's self by means of an apostrophe is a very common thing in these days."

"Well, look at this pocket-book. Here is a marquis's cornet, and a capital A; that is to say, Marquis d'Argental."

"What! you think that this case belonged—"

"To our friend Pierre. And now I understand his death. He was killed by some one who wished to regain possession of the letters he kept in this case. So the crime was committed, or at least instigated, by a woman."

"I admire your bold reasoning, though I think it decidedly paradoxical. The scoundrel who stole this pocket-book would not have thrown it into our cab."

"You told me yourself that he was closely followed by two persons who seemed to be watching him. He perhaps feared that he would be arrested and searched; and he did not know that we were intimate with Dargental. He thought that we should keep the pocket-book, and burn the letters which could be of no possible interest to us, and which he was anxious to get rid of at any cost."

"Then, according to you, that man intended to return these letters to the various women they compromised. You must admit that this supposition is absurd in the extreme."

"Oh! he was only acting on behalf of *one* of the women."

"Which one? There are three letters, but each of them is written in a different hand. You said so yourself."

"I may have been mistaken. I think I will examine them more closely. Let us take a seat in front of that café. I see a table in a corner where we shall be comparatively alone."

George Caumont assented to the proposal, and as soon as the friends were seated in a little niche in front of the Café Américain, Puymirol opened the pocket-book. "Let us proceed systematically," he remarked. "Here is the first letter. It is not long, but it is expressive. 'My adored one,' it says, 'I am ready to leave everything to follow you, and to sacrifice, for your sake, all that I prize most in this world, my children and my good name. When shall we start? Say the word, and I will join you. Take me to the end of the world, and make me your slave. I shall be only too happy, for I cannot live apart from you.' I have skipped the kisses. There are too many of them," concluded Adhémar, sneering.

"My children!" repeated George, ironically. "Then Blanche certainly did not write that letter. She has no children."

"Nor has Madame de Lescombat any. But let us examine the next missive: 'My friend, I have loved you, I love you still; but if you go on in this way, I shall no longer love you. I shall even hate you, and I do not conceal from you that there lurks in my heart a feeling that you would do well not to arouse. Have you ever seen Sardou's "Hatred" played? Well, I am a Florentine Parisienne, and I should know how to avenge my wrongs, as Italian women revenged theirs in the middle ages. These are no meaningless threats, my dear. To extricate you from a terrible predicament I once committed an act that might have sent me straight to the Assizes, and I mean to be rewarded by your devotion. You must choose between her and me. You understand me, do you not? I await in reply, not words, but acts. I shall expect you to-morrow, you bad fellow, whom I love so much. Bring me what you swore to return to me, or there will be bitter war.'"

"The deuce!" exclaimed George, "that woman doesn't bandy

words. I should think her quite capable of conniving at Dargental's murder to regain possession of a letter in which she owns that she had committed a crime. She does not state what crime, but she may have committed forgery; and if Dargental profited by the deed, as she says clearly enough, he certainly had good reason to fear her vengeance."

"Then, if this letter came from Blanche Pornic, you would be inclined to think that the murder was committed by her orders, and for her benefit?"

"I would not swear that such was the case; but it would seem very probable."

"Well, I know her; and I am sure that she was the writer of this threatening missive. 'You must choose between her and me.' 'Her' is Madame de Lescombat, her rival; and I would wager almost any amount that the letter is not a week old. A day or two after it was written, Dargental's intended marriage was announced. He had refused to fulfil his promise, and Blanche avenged herself accordingly."

"But if they had quarrelled to that point, he would not have invited her to lunch with us this morning."

"There is nothing to prove that she did not invite herself, in order to throw us off the track. But let us pass on to the third letter." So saying, Puymirol drew it from the pocket-book, unfolded it, and uttered an exclamation of astonishment. "What is the matter?" asked George.

Puymirol, instead of replying, proceeded to unfold the telegram, which he had drawn from his pocket, with the Russian leather case, and spread it out upon the table beside the third letter, which he had not yet read. "This last missive certainly comes from Madame de Lescombat," he grunted. "The handwriting is precisely the same as that of the telegraphic note."

"Then Madame de Lescombat was probably as deeply interested as her rivals in regaining possession of her correspondence. You must admit that."

"Yes; but as Dargental was about to marry her, he would have returned her the letter, had she desired it."

"Who knows? Read it, and let me know your opinion afterwards."

Puymirol complied, though somewhat reluctantly, for he was afraid he would be obliged to change his first opinion. He read as follows: "'My king, my love, my life, I am intoxicated with happiness. What blissful hours I have spent with you! When will they return? Why did I allow you to depart? I feel a mad desire to hasten after you, and throw myself in the arms that clasped me so fondly. Before I met you I never knew what it was to love. Now, however, my happiness is perfect, and I have proved to you how ardent is my affection. I have placed myself in your power by confiding my great secret to you. In a word, you might ruin me. And if I write this, it is in order that you may have in your possession a proof, a confession. If I deceived you, if I ceased to love you— But I am blaspheming! I shall love you until my latest breath. But if I ever give you any cause of complaint, show me no mercy, crush me, deliver me up; I shall have deserved my fate. Oh, when will the day come when I shall be able to acknowledge you as my lord and master before all the world? When shall I bear your name? It seems to me that day will never come. Eight months longer to wait! Eight months during which we must conceal our love, and pretend to mourn a being I loathed. And what if you learned to love another in the meantime? What if your infatuation should return for the woman I hate the most because it was she whom you most loved. Ah! I should die. It would kill me; but I should not die without being avenged upon that creature.'"

"Well, what do you think of that?" asked George.

"I think that the lady was desperately in love with Dargental, and that she was out of her mind when she wrote that letter."

"It was evidently written just two months after her husband's death, for she deplores the fact that her happiness must be deferred eight months longer, and the law does not allow a woman to marry again until ten months of widowhood have expired."

"But it is at the least two years since Lescombat died of apoplexy."

"Or of something else. Well, the marriage was deferred for some reason or other, which is conclusive proof that the courtship was stormy. The countess has had plenty of time to change her mind."

"She did not change it, as she meant to marry Dargental next week."

"I admit that; but perhaps she was not so much in earnest as formerly. Dargental, in spite of his promises, had not severed his connection with Blanche Pornic, and Madame de Lescombat may have regretted saying, and above all, writing, so much; she herself could not break the engagement, as he had her completely in his power."

"And you fancy that she could devise no other means but murder to escape him. That is absurd, my dear fellow."

"Less absurd than your suspicions respecting Blanche, for this letter is certainly from the countess; and we are by no means sure that the other comes from the actress." Puymirol hung his head. He was obliged to confess that George was right, though it cost him a struggle to admit it. "However, I don't see," added Caumont, "why we should devote our attention to this mystery. The authorities will take charge of that. You have only to hand the letters to the commissary of police, and state how you came into possession of them."

"I shall not do that," said Adhémar quickly. "I don't want to inform on any one."

"But you talk about avenging Dargental's death."

"Quite so, and when I learn who the guilty party is, I will decide on my course. I shall begin my search after the truth to-morrow. Before doing so, however, I want to know the result of the inquiry now in progress."

"How will you learn that result?"

"We shall be summoned as witnesses; and the questions put to us will indicate how the magistrate views the affair. But we can not stay here forever. Shall we go to the club? Balmer will be there by about four o'clock; and there are some questions that I should like to ask him. He was very intimate with Dargental, so he may be able to enlighten me respecting certain circumstances."

The two friends thereupon rose up and repaired to their club, a second-rate establishment in the Avenue de l'Opéra hard by. They had been elected members, thanks to Dargental. On arriving, they found that Balmer had not yet put in an appearance, so they sat down in a corner to wait for him. Their thoughts followed very different channels. Puymirol, while regretting Dargental, to whom he was indebted for many little services, hoped to profit by his death, without knowing exactly how. He had, however, more ambition than scruples, and though he would not have stooped to blackmailing, he did not hesitate about fishing in muddy waters. He said to himself that Madame de Lescombat, whether innocent or guilty of the murder, would give almost anything to regain possession of her letter, and that she would be disposed to assist any man who might restore it to her; now, why should he not be the man? These intentions were certainly not very laudable; but when a fellow wishes to succeed at any cost, he must not be over fastidious. Caumont, on his side, did not feel the slightest interest in the countess, and had only undertaken Blanche Pornic's defence from a sense of justice. He had never liked Dargental, though he had seen a good deal of him, having been dragged into his society by Puymirol. He regretted his untimely death, but felt no desire to avenge it; indeed, he was sorry that he had become mixed up in the affair of the pocket-book and the letters. In point of fact, he had other thoughts in his mind. He had recently met a young lady whom he greatly admired, and whom he wished to marry.

While the two friends thus sat side by side on a sofa, smoking in silence, Charles Balmer suddenly appeared looking considerably excited. "Do you know what has happened?" he asked, in a husky voice. "I have just come from Dargental's."

"We went there in advance of you. He is dead," said Adhémar.

"He was murdered, my dear fellow. I fell into a nest of detectives, magistrates, and physicians, and I thought for a while that they were going to arrest me. They confined themselves to questioning me, however."

"Have they discovered the culprit?" asked Adhémar.

"Well, they have arrested the valet, who stoutly denies any knowledge of the crime. I know him, and I would stake my life upon his innocence. Besides, Dargental's pocket-book was stolen, and it certainly was not Jean who took it, for he was searched, and only thirty-seven sous were found upon him. They are going to keep him in jail, all the same, but I am convinced that his innocence will be established sooner or later on."

"But how do they know that the pocket-book was stolen?"

"Dargental always carried it in his breast-pocket. Jean himself told the commissary so, and the pocket was empty. Poor Pierre! when I think how we blamed him for keeping us waiting! He was just starting off to lunch with us when he was killed—by whom, no one can tell." With these words Balmer left the two friends to approach the card tables and inform the other members present of the violent death which had befallen one of the boldest players of the club.

"Well," said George to Puymirol, "after what you have just heard, do you still persist in your determination to usurp the functions of the police?"

"I not only persist in my determination, but I shall begin work this very evening," replied Adhémar, taking up his hat. "You can return home if you like; I mean to call on the countess."

## II.

Every April the horse-show, held annually at the Palais de l'Industrie in the Champs Elysées, is one of the favourite resorts of Parisian society; and on the day when the chargers parade, ridden by lieutenants and sub-lieutenants, quite prepared to break their necks in order to attract the attention of the ladies, a large crowd is invariably present. The attractive gathering took place that year a fortnight after Dargental's tragical demise. Both George Caumont and Adhémar de Puymirol were there, having met each other by appointment at the door. Since their friend's death they had not seen nearly so much of each other as usual. They still lived in the same house, and upon the same floor, but in the morning, instead of going out together as formerly, each of them went his own way, for George had refused to help Adhémar in discovering the murderer, and spent his time in a manner more congenial to his tastes. The fact that Dargental had not committed suicide was now established, but, otherwise, no progress had been made with the investigation. The valet was still in prison, but stoutly protested his innocence, and there was really no evidence against him. Puymirol, who might have furnished a clue as to the truth, remained obstinately silent. Upon being questioned by the magistrate, on the day following the crime, he had contented himself with relating the incidents of the lunch. George Caumont had been equally reticent, and so had Balmer and Blanche Pornic, who were also questioned; and as the valet persisted in his denials, it would be necessary to set him at liberty sooner or later.

Puymirol's attempts to obtain an interview with the countess had proved utterly fruitless. Madame de Lescombat received no one, and this was only natural, after the tragical event which had bereft her of her betrothed. A letter which Puymirol had written to her, requesting a private interview, had remained unanswered, and our amateur detective, greatly vexed, was, therefore, reduced to waiting for an opportunity which might never present itself. On trying to console himself by card-playing, he met with a terrible run of ill luck; and finding himself most embarrassed, it is no wonder if he felt dreadfully out of sorts as he strolled that day on Caumont's arm through the crowd inside the Palais de l'Industrie. George, on his side, seemed to be eyeing the occupants of the benches as if in search of some acquaintance. Indeed, he suddenly let go of his friend's arm, and Puymirol exclaimed: "Ah! there's your sweetheart—Well, go and see her. We will meet here during the intermission that follows the hurdle race."

"I can not promise to be punctual," replied Caumont, evidently anxious to start off.

In another moment he could be seen cautiously making his way towards a remarkably charming girl, who sat with her friends in one of the tribunes: but he seemed to be in no hurry to reach her, for he often paused as he approached the staircase, which he would have to ascend. He was not far from it when the young lady recognised him and smiled. He thereupon eagerly bowed, blushing a little as he did so, and then, quickening his pace, he began to elbow his way through the crowd—no easy task. Just then, however, he found himself, to his surprise, face to face with Blanche Pornic. The meeting was very disagreeable to George, who knew that the eyes of the girl he admired were upon him, so he endeavoured to turn a little aside and thus avoid Blanche, but she resolutely barred his way. "I see that you are not particularly glad to meet me," she remarked, laughing, "but I shall inflict my society upon you to punish you for failing to call on me as you promised."

"I did very wrong, I admit," replied George, "and I will atone for my fault to-morrow; but you will excuse me for leaving you now, as I must join a friend who is waiting for me."

"He will have to wait then, for you can't go any further as another trial is about to take place. Don't you hear the bell?" Blanche spoke the truth. The promenaders, warned by the signal, had paused, and any further progress was impossible. "I have you," she continued, "and I sha'n't let you go, for I want to have a long talk with you about Dargental's death."

George resolved to make the best of the situation, so he replied: "Well, as you insist upon broaching that sad subject, it is said that Dargental did not commit suicide as was at first supposed."

"No doubt," replied Blanche. "Suicide was far from his thoughts. He was murdered, my dear fellow, and I believe I know the culprit."

George had not expected to hear the person whom Puymirol suspected of the crime make such a statement as this. "You know the culprit and yet you have not denounced him," said he.

"Oh! I make it a principle never to meddle with matters that don't concern me."

"But this does concern you. You knew Dargental so well."

"No doubt; and he has died for having deserted me."

"I don't understand you."

"Oh! that doesn't matter. Had I cared to tell what I know, I should have done so to the magistrate who questioned me; and I deserve some credit for holding my tongue, for he insinuated that suspicion might fall upon me. But I have nothing to fear, and I am going to stand my ground. Have you seen the Countess de Lescombat?" added Blanche, abruptly, "I suppose you know she is here."

"Here, a fortnight after Dargental's death? It's impossible!"

"She is enthroned up there in the stewards' stand, and Dargental's death has not affected her in the least."

"It is certainly scandalous," replied George.

"Oh! she imagines that by showing herself here, she will make people believe that Dargental was indifferent to her."

"But all Paris knew of the connection, and she was about to legalise it by marriage."

"We knew it, but the banns had not been published, and Madame de Lescombat will now declare that Pierre was a friend, and nothing more. And people will end by believing that such was really the case, unless some of her letters should be found among the poor fellow's papers, But she is too shrewd to write. It is all very well for me who have nothing to lose to be prodigal with my signature. If Dargental has not burned my letters, an interesting collection will be found."

"Dargental probably destroyed them; still, it isn't likely that they contained anything that would compromise you," said George, scrutinizing Blanche's countenance.

"Well," replied Blanche, quite composed, "I never concealed my fondness for Pierre, and I did for him what I would never have done for any other living being. But when I learned to know him well, I deeply regretted writing him a certain note, which might cause me a deal of trouble, should it fall into the hands of the authorities. Dargental was quite capable of keeping this note. I begged of him to return it to me before his marriage, and if I accepted his invitation at the Lion d'Or, it was because I hoped he would return it to me at dessert."

"But in what way could this note compromise you?" inquired George, trying to smile. "I presume that it didn't contain a confession of any crime on your part."

"You know nothing about women," replied Blanche. "The very best of them are fools when their affections are involved, and I was madly in love with Dargental. To save him from any danger, I would have stolen or committed murder, but I did not go to such lengths as that; still I did him a service that might have cost me dear. I tell you this, because I know I can trust you; but, pray, say nothing to your friend Puymirol about the matter, for I have no confidence in him. He sides with the countess, and I am almost certain that he just left you to go and pay his respects to her. But what do you think of the show this year?"

"It is about the same as usual, I fancy."

"You wonder why I came, probably. Well, I came here to see the officers. Like all the rest of my sex, I am fond of uniforms. There is one officer here whom I have taken a special fancy to. Shall I point him out to you?"

"Certainly," replied George, although he was not at all interested in the matter.

"Step here a moment, then," said Blanche. A hurdle trial was now taking place, and as the different competitors passed by, she indulged in lively criticism. "There he is, at last," she continued, pointing to a young sub-lieutenant and then clapping her hands like a child, she added: "Isn't he handsome?"

George looked at the rider, who had excited her admiration, and beheld a tall, well-built young man, with a handsome and genial face, mounted upon a half-bred horse, which he managed with wonderful skill and ease. "Do you know who he is?" Caumont asked of Blanche.

"No; but I should very much like to know. If he does not receive the first prize, the judges will be guilty of the grossest injustice. Did you notice him bow to these ladies over there, that young girl in a lace bonnet, with an older lady, who must have been very handsome, and who still has some good looks left her?" George glanced in the direction indicated, and, on recognising the ladies, blushed so deeply that Blanche resumed: "So they are friends of yours? You need not blush like a schoolboy, for they are both charming, the girl especially, and I am delighted that you know them; for now you can introduce the lieutenant to me."

"You had better not count upon that," retorted George, drily.

"Oh! you need not take offence, I meant no harm. You seem to be deeply interested in one of the two ladies; and I should never forgive myself if I prevented you from following the dictates of your heart any longer. So go, and good luck to you!"

George now thought of reaching the tribune to join the ladies who interested him far more than Blanche Pornic's revelations. The trial was over, the judges had retired for deliberation, and Caumont was about to climb the stairs when he perceived the people he wished to join coming down towards him. The daughter was in front, and she smiled as he stood, with uncovered head, eagerly awaiting her approach. He had been introduced to herself and her mother by an old schoolmate of his, now a civil engineer, who had informed him that Madame Verdon was the widow of an iron manufacturer who had left a fortune of twelve hundred thousand francs, which would revert, partly to his son and partly to his daughter, Gabrielle, the young girl who was now descending the stairs. George had often met her and her mother in the Luxembourg gardens and had visited them at their residence on the Boulevard St. Michel, very near his own abode. He had gradually fallen in love with Mademoiselle Verdon, but being well aware of the objections that might be made to him as a suitor for the hand of a young lady blessed with an income of twenty thousand francs, he had carefully abstained from playing the part of a lover. Still, he had eyes, and he saw very plainly that the daughter liked him, and that the mother did not seem to discourage his pretensions. He even fancied that Madame Verdon had been unusually cordial of late, and he wondered if the time had not come for him to make some advances. He wished, however, first to have an explanation with the young girl, and then if he met with any encouragement from her, to ask her hand of her mother. But a favourable opportunity had not yet presented itself. Indeed, Dargental's death, and the judicial proceedings following upon that tragical event, had, for some days, engrossed George's attention to such an extent that he had scarcely seen the Verdons. "Good-morning," exclaimed the mother, as she now approached. "We haven't seen you for a long time past. What have you been doing with yourself? Gabrielle has lost all fondness for the Luxembourg garden since you have ceased visiting it."

"Yes, monsieur," chimed in the young girl, "it is very unkind of you to desert us, and your conduct is inexcusable, for it cannot be your law studies that engross you, as you spend your time here."

"It is the first time I have been here this year, mademoiselle."

"Oh! I am not scolding you. It is much more amusing here than in our quiet neighbourhood, especially for you who are probably acquainted with all these people. I, myself, have eyes only for my brother."

"Your brother, mademoiselle?"

"Yes," replied Madame Verdon, "my son, Albert, has just taken part in one of the trials, and as I am confident that he will receive the first prize, I came here expressly to enjoy his triumph. You must allow me to introduce him to you when the awards have been made. He has a three months' leave, which he will spend with us."

"I thought your son was still at Saint Cyr," stammered George.

"He has been promoted to sub-lieutenancy in the Seventh Cuirassiers. This promotion makes me feel very old, I assure you; and I must confess that I am rather averse to admitting that I have a son who is twenty-six years of age."

"You will see how handsome my big brother is," interrupted Gabrielle. "All the ladies applauded him enthusiastically when he jumped the last hurdle. The one who was talking with you must have split her gloves in her fervour."

George said nothing, but he blushed to his very ears. He had flattered himself that Gabrielle Verdon had not noticed his long conversation with Blanche Pornic, but he could no longer delude himself on the point. "Doesn't your father ever come to Paris, now?" inquired Madame Verdon. "He must be very fond of horses?"

"My father is getting too old to travel about much," replied George, somewhat astonished by this remark.

"I understand. When a person has charge of a large estate, it is difficult for him to absent himself. An estate is like an iron foundry: it needs constant attention. I know something about that, for I spent ten years in the valley of the Vosges. My husband only took me to Paris once a year. You scarcely remember that time, child. Monsieur Jacques has not forgotten it, however." These concluding words were evidently addressed to a gentleman whom George had not before noticed, but whom Madame Verdon now disclosed to view by stepping a little aside. This person was tall, broad shouldered, and stoutly built. His rather coarse features gave him a stern air, and he was wanting in elegance of manner, although he was very neatly dressed. "Let me introduce Monsieur Jacques Rochas, my husband's former partner, and his successor," resumed Madame Verdon. "He has just sold the iron works he purchased from us, and has come to reside in Paris. You will meet him frequently at our house."

George bowed coldly, and the stranger returned the salute in a somewhat bearish fashion. Both gentlemen seemed ill at ease, and Madame Verdon herself appeared rather uncomfortable. "Here are the victors now," cried Gabrielle. "Albert leads the procession. Let us get a little nearer to see the party form. Use your elbows, Monsieur George, and make room for us through the crowd." And without troubling herself as to whether her mother was following her or not, she turned to the left, followed by George, who asked no better than to have a private interview with the young girl.

"Madame Verdon will think I am running away with you," he said, jestingly.

"We shall be able to find her again presently, without any trouble," replied Gabrielle. "She doesn't worry herself much about me just now. Here is a good place for a quiet talk, and I wish to speak to you upon a serious subject."

"I am entirely at your service, mademoiselle," replied George, who was greatly astonished.

The musicians now struck up a triumphal march, and, amid the din, Gabrielle resumed: "I warn you that I am going to ask you a very strange and improper question. You have been paying me considerable attention of late. Do you love me?"

This question was indeed unexpected—the more so as well-bred young ladies habitually wait for it to be put to them. Mademoiselle Verdon was certainly reversing the usual order of things; but George promptly answered: "Love you, mademoiselle! yes, with my whole heart. I have not yet dared to tell you so, but—"

"No protestations. I believe you, and I am going to enable

you to prove the truth of your words. Do you wish to marry me?"

"Such is my most ardent desire. If I could hope that your mother would grant me your hand—"

"She will, if you ask her for it now; that is to say, within a few days. Later on, she will, perhaps, refuse you." George could not understand the meaning of all this, as his bewildered mien showed plainly enough. "The situation is simply this," continued Gabrielle: "My mother wishes to marry again. This news may surprise you, but it is true, nevertheless. She wishes to marry again, to enter society. Her children are in her way, and she does not at all care to keep them with her. My brother does not so much preoccupy her. An officer goes about from garrison to garrison when he is not in the field, so she will seldom see Albert; but as I cannot leave her as long as I remain single, she is in a hurry to get me married off. She is looking for a husband for me, and if you do not speak out she will content herself with the first comer."

"Oh! she will easily secure a much more eligible suitor than myself, for I have neither money nor prospects."

"I have money enough for two, and your future depends upon your intelligence and industry. My mother knows this perfectly well; she also knows that I like you. Moreover, she has made inquiries respecting you. She has received information that your family is highly respectable, and that your father will leave you his estate and some capital. She is in a hurry to settle the matter, for you see it would not do for both the mother and the daughter to marry within a few days of each other. She dreads ridicule, and she is quite right, for all our acquaintances would laugh at her. But if I now became your wife, she would trouble herself no further about me. She would leave Paris, and, after travelling awhile, she would be married in Switzerland or Italy. She told me yesterday that she wished to leave next month, and that she did not want to take me with her. The only refuge left for me would be a convent, for I cannot follow Albert's regiment about, and he is my only relative." George was so overwhelmed by these disclosures, that he did not know what to reply, and Gabrielle concluded that he did not care for her. "I see that you are shocked to hear me talk in this way," she said, sadly. "I know I do wrong in censuring my mother's conduct in your presence, and throwing myself in your arms, as it were. But I never could disguise my feelings, and I always speak straight to the point. I thought you loved me well enough to do me justice. If I am mistaken I must bear the penalty of my imprudence; but you at least cannot accuse me of dissimulation."

"On the contrary, I sincerely thank you, mademoiselle, for divining the feelings which I dared not express, and I entreat you not to take my silence as a sign of coldness or hesitation. My delight overcame me. I was so little prepared for the happiness you have announced to me."

"It is not my fault if I did not explain the situation sooner. I have not seen you for several days. But, now, will you authorise me to inform my mother that you intend to ask for my hand in marriage—at an early date?"

"To-morrow, if I have your consent, mademoiselle."

"Thank you," replied the girl, earnestly. "I can never do enough to prove to you my love and gratitude. My brother will be as pleased as I am when I introduce you to him by-and-by. They are very slow in forming the procession, it seems to me," continued Gabrielle. "They have no right to keep a sister waiting so long for her brother's triumphal entry."

"Nor a mother who is longing to applaud her son," added George, in a somewhat questioning tone.

"Mamma? Oh, yes, she is fond of Albert, but she will wait quite contentedly, as her intended husband is with her."

"Her intended husband?"

"Ah! I forgot to tell you that she expects to marry the person she just introduced to you, Monsieur Jacques Rochas."

"Your father's former partner?"

"That is the title my mother gives him. The truth is, he was formerly a foreman at the iron works. He subsequently became superintendent, and, after my father's death, he leased the works. He made a good deal of money, and finally purchased the place from us. It seems that he has just disposed of it very advantageously, and is now much richer than we are."

"But it cannot be for the sake of his money that your mother wishes to marry him?"

"No, though my father only left her one fourth of his property. She likes Monsieur Rochas, but, for myself, I cannot imagine what attraction she can possibly find in a man who has a very limited education, and whom she formerly regarded as an inferior. He looks very like a farrier, and he is stern and gloomy, as well as taciturn."

"I noticed that he did not greet me very cordially just now. I am inclined to think that he will not approve of our marriage."

"You are very much mistaken there. He suspects that I don't like him, and he is anxious to separate me from my mother. It matters very little to him whom I marry, providing I cease to live with her. He wishes to be absolute master in his own house, and probably thinks that I might rebel against his authority."

"But what does your brother say to Madame Verdon's plans?"

"Oh! I am sure that he will be furious when she announces her intended marriage to him. He will certainly try to dissuade her, but he won't succeed, for she has engaged herself to this man, and she is really afraid of him. But there is my brother Albert passing now." And so saying, Gabrielle raised herself on tiptoe, and with her gloved hand began to shower kisses upon the young officer, who seemed blind to this exhibition of sisterly affection. In fact, he appeared to be gazing with extraordinary persistence at somebody whom George could not see. Just then, too, the young lieutenant dexterously caught a little bunch of violets that was sent flying at him through the air; he smiled at the sender of this fragrant missile, and then, giving his horse the rein, galloped off without even seeming to suspect that his mother and sister were present. "Didn't I tell you that he was turning all the women's heads?" whispered Gabrielle to George. "He is so handsome! But I should like to get a look at his latest victim."

This wish was promptly gratified, for, just then, the crowd divided to allow Blanche Pornic to pass. She had a triumphant air, and the smile with which she had just favoured the young lieutenant was still upon her lips. "Why, it is the same person whom you were talking with when we came down the steps," remarked Gabrielle. "I am afraid she has bewitched my brother. Did you notice that he kept the bouquet of violets she flung at him? But here is my mother coming with Monsieur Rochas. If she were alone, I should beg of you to remain with us; but this gentleman's presence would not prove congenial to you, so take leave of my mother, and meet us in the Luxembourg garden to-morrow. We shall be there at four o'clock."

George took his leave as Gabrielle suggested and was about to turn away, when a hand was placed on his shoulder, and on looking round, he found himself face to face with Charles Balmer. "I have found you at last!" exclaimed the latter. "I have some news for you about Dargental's case. Poor Pierre's valet has spoken at last."

"How do you know?" inquired George.

"Why, I am intimate with the magistrate to whom the investigation of the case is entrusted, and he tells me that Jean now remembers, that at about nine o'clock on the morning of the murder, a rather suspicious-looking man rang at the door. Jean answered the bell, and this man, who seemed greatly annoyed on seeing him, asked for some person whom Jean had never heard of. He then said that he must have made a mistake in the number of the house, and went off without insisting any further. Ten minutes later, Dargental, having completed his toilet, sent Jean to Madame de Lescombat's with a letter, and Jean, as he left the house, saw the same man standing in a doorway on the opposite side of the street. He thought very little about it at the time, but started off on his errand. The countess resides at some distance from Dargental's house; besides, our friend had given Jean several other commissions, which explains why he failed to return until you and Puymirol reached the scene of the catastrophe. The fact is, that strange man must have seen Jean leave the house, and then, realising that our unfortunate friend was alone, he went upstairs again, whereupon Dargental himself must have opened the door."

"No doubt; but to what motive does the magistrate ascribe the crime?"

"To robbery, as Dargental's pocket-book is missing."

"But are you sure that this pocket-book contained any money?"

"One cannot be sure, of course, but it seems more than probable. Dargental was in the habit of carrying all the money he possessed about him, and Jean declares that his master, on going to bed at night, always placed his pocket-book under the bolster. Besides, all the drawers have been carefully examined, and not a penny has been found in the place."

"And no article of furniture was forced open by the murderer?"

"None, whatever. He evidently knew exactly where to look for what he wanted. Besides, he was probably anxious to get away as soon as possible, as some one might have come in at any moment. It seems that the only clue the authorities possess consists of a memorandum in Dargental's handwriting which was found in the ante-room. The murderer must have dropped it on opening the pocket-book, for the imprint of his bloody fingers is visible on one corner of it."

"And what is this memorandum?"

"Robergeot would not tell me—Robergeot is the magistrate. He has great confidence in me, as he has known me from my infancy; but he has a very keen sense of professional duty, so that all I have been able to learn is that the note in question may prove of great use in discovering the criminal. I certainly hope the brigand will be apprehended, for if the murder of my friend Dargental should go unpunished, I believe I shall really die a year before my time, and that would upset all my calculations, for I still have money enough left to last me thirty months longer."

"Ah, yes, I forgot that you were a chronic consumptive," said George ironically. "Poor fellow! However, if this is all you have to tell me—"

"Yes, for the time being; but I shall see Robergeot again, and I will keep you well informed, though you don't seem to take much interest in the affair. You are not like Puymirol. He knows that I am acquainted with the magistrate, and he asks me every day how the investigation is progressing. But speaking of Puymirol, are you aware that he lost five hundred louis more at cards last night?"

"No, I just left him, but he said nothing to me about it," murmured George, surprised and still more annoyed at this news. "Perhaps he has not gone off yet. I am going to wait for him at the door."

"That means, you have had enough of my company, so I will leave you."

George was now anxious to see Puymirol, for he felt that his friend had no right to keep a pocket-book and letters which might put the authorities on the right scent, for he did not believe that the robbery of any money had had anything to do with the crime. Moreover, he wished to ask Adhémar how he was situated financially, and ascertain if this last loss of ten thousand francs would not prove an irreparable misfortune as he greatly feared. He therefore hurried to the grand entrance where there was a dense crowd, at sight of which he almost despaired of finding Puymirol. However, luck favoured him, but, first, he saw Blanche Pornic pass out, accompanied by a young officer who was none other than Albert Verdon. She did not stop to speak to George, but she gave him a mocking smile as she passed by. She had succeeded in her purpose; the young lieutenant to whom she had taken such a fancy, had evidently been impressed by her charms. George had not time to think over the matter, for just then, Puymirol, coming upon him unexpectedly, caught hold of his arm, and dragged him off, exclaiming: "I want you to do me a favour."

"Nothing would give me greater pleasure, but I have not got the amount you lost at the club last night," replied George.

"That isn't the question. I have at last succeeded in securing a few moments' conversation with the countess, and I am now going to see her at her house, where we shall probably have a decisive interview. Her letter is a weapon which I have resolved to use, but I don't want to have it about me during my first visit, so do me the favour to keep the pocket-book for me until to-morrow."

"Dargental's pocket-book! Not if I know it!"

"So you are afraid of compromising yourself. Very well, merely take the letters, then." And Puymirol, as he spoke, drew all three of them out of the compartment in which they had been placed, and, after thrusting them into George Caumont's hand, hastened rapidly away.

## III.

THE Countess de Lescombat's residence on the Boulevard de Courcelles was an imposing structure which, in Italy, would certainly have been styled the Lescombat Palace. Standing majestically between a large court-yard and spacious grounds, this seigneurial mansion seemed intended to accommodate some exiled king. M. de Lescombat, who had erected this residence, had been a *blasé* sceptic, knowing no law save his own caprice. After amusing himself for several years, he had crowned his career as an eccentric millionaire by marrying the pretended ward of a middle class libertine, a certain Octavia Crochard, whose story had been accurately related by Blanche Pornic, the actress. The result of this marriage was that M. de Lescombat suddenly took his departure for a better world after bequeathing his entire fortune to his wife, and whatever Blanche might say to the contrary, it was scarcely likely that he had committed suicide, for he had certainly had every reason to desire to remain alive. However, the countess, as soon as she became a widow, behaved with the utmost tact. She retained the services of the old Marchioness de Monastier, a dowager who had long assisted the count in doing the honours of his princely mansion, and who was now quite willing to act as chaperon to his widow;

and a most complaisant chaperon she proved, winking at such secret peccadillos as Octavia indulged in. The countess now meant to lead a quiet, independent life, but a woman's plans are rarely carried out. Shortly after her husband's death, Dargental was introduced to her by a mutual friend, and she soon became so infatuated with him, that she promised to marry him at the expiration of the ten months' delay prescribed by law.

This promise had failed to take effect, as her intended husband had been taken from her by a most terrible, unforeseen catastrophe. It may be asked, how had she borne this terrible blow? Madame de Monastier alone conld have answered the question, for since Dargental's death Madame de Lescombat had not left her house, and he had been buried without her showing herself at the funeral. Moreover, all Puymirol's efforts to enter into communication with her had proved unavailing. Everything seemed to indicate that she meant to let a suitable interval elapse before she emerged from seclusion, and, indeed, when Puymirol met her at the horse show it was the first time that she had appeared in public since her lover's death. She had thought it an excellent opportunity to let people understand that she had no intention of immuring herself forever, and so she had repaired to the Palais de l'Industrie in a toilet suited to the occasion. She there received the friends who approached her with perfect serenity, and cut their expressions of condolence short by a few well-chosen words.

Puymirol knew her but slightly. Dargental had taken him to two or three of her entertainments, and as he was a superb waltzer she had noticed him at the time; but he feared that she had now well-nigh forgotten him, and that she would pay no more attention to his remarks than she had paid to his letters. He was thus agreeably surprised when he saw her smile upon him in the most engaging manner while he approached the tribune where she was seated. He then stationed himself at the foot of the staircase, and, deciding to bide his time, waited for the countess's departure, when he might have an opportunity of saying a few words to her in private. Indeed, when the show was about to close for the day, the countess descended the steps, and leaving the two or three gentlemen who were in obsequious attendance upon her, came straight towards him, apologized for not having received him at her house, and inquired if it would suit him to come and see her that very afternoon. Puymirol eagerly accepted the invitation, although her unexpected cordiality aroused his distrust. However, on catching sight of George, he forthwith determined to place the letters in his keeping as a precaution against a fascination he feared. He reached the countess's house but a quarter of an hour after her own return, and a footman at once escorted him through a suite of magnificent apartments to the boudoir where the lovely widow usually received her intimate friends. He found her armed for conquest. She was certainly a superb creature. Tall, with faultless shoulders, she had a head like that of a Grecian statue, and her white brow was crowned with heavy coils of ruddy hair, of the tint which the Venetian masters were so fond of. Puymirol seated himself in a low chair near her, and was wondering how he should open the conversation when, without any preamble, she exclaimed: "Let us talk of poor Pierre, shall we not?"

"Pierre Dargental?" said Puymirol. "Yes, that was what brought me here."

This was only partially true, however, for he admired the countess exceedingly, and, besides, now that he was in her presence, he experienced the wonderful charm that she exercised over all the men who approached her. She, no doubt, realised it, for, fixing her large green eyes, full of a strange fire, upon him, she softly said: "I thought you had called partially on my account."

"And you are right," exclaimed Puymirol, impulsively.

"Then I forgive you for your almost rude remark. We are already old friends, you and I, for it was more than a year ago that poor Pierre introduced you to me. Do you recollect the ball at which you led the cotillon?"

"I remember it as if it were but yesterday."

"And so do I, for I have never met your equal as a waltzer since. But you have made no effort to see me since last winter."

"I feared annoying Dargental."

"Yes, he was terribly jealous, but, poor fellow, I forgive him. His terrible death has been a sad blow for me. I see by your face that you don't believe that—no doubt, because you saw me at the show just now in a spring toilet. However, a woman is not obliged to put on a black dress to be deeply afflicted. My heart is in mourning, but I don't deem it necessary to publish my grief."

"Oh, I don't presume to criticise you, madame. On the contrary, I bless the chance that brought about a meeting between us, for you have repeatedly refused me an interview."

"I treated everyone alike. I even thought strongly of leaving Paris for a few months, but I finally came to the conclusion that absence would not cure my grief, and I summoned up courage to shake off the prostration to which my loss had reduced me."

"I trusted that you would at least reply to the letter in which I begged of you to grant me an interview."

"You must not be offended with me on account of my failure to do so. I never write to any one. It is against my principles."

"But you must break this rule sometimes," said Adhémar, gazing searchingly at the countess.

"Not often," was the calm response. "My autograph letters ought to fetch a good price, for there are certainly very few of them."

"It would, doubtless, surprise you very much if I told you that I have one in my possession."

"Indeed! I should really like to see it."

"Well, I regret that I haven't got it with me. I should add, however, that it is a very unimportant document; the telegraphic note you sent to Pierre at the Lion d'Or."

"Yes! I recollect that. But I cannot imagine how you came by it."

"Poor Dargental was dead when it was delivered. We were ignorant of the fact, and were breakfasting without him, at the time, and Charles Balmer, who was one of the guests, took the liberty to open the message and show it to us."

"That doesn't surprise me. Monsieur Balmer is always doing something stupid. But I am surprised you kept it."

"I meant to hand it to Dargental as soon as the lunch was over. But, alas! I arrived at his place too late."

"Yes," murmured Madame de Lescombat. "I know the terrible story."

"I should have returned the note to you if I had been able to see you, and I will return it now whenever you like, but I have read and re-read it many times, and I now know your writing as well as if I had received hundreds of letters from you."

"And what do you think of the contents of this famous missive?"

"I think you were most kind and indulgent as regards poor Pierre in letting him invite to that lunch—"

"Some of his old flames. Well, I felt tolerably sure of him, but in my secret heart I was a trifle anxious, as you may judge from the fact that I begged him to come and see me as soon as the repast was over. How many ladies were present?"

"Only one, Blanche Pornic."

"Ah! he had sworn never to see her again," sighed Octavia. "It grieves me to think she was there. She nearly ruined poor Pierre. I succeeded in getting him out of her clutches, and she has never forgiven me for it. She, no doubt, spoke about me during the lunch?"

"Yes, madame, and I won't conceal from you the fact that she isn't very kindly disposed towards you."

"Oh, I can guess what she said about me. She told you that I was the daughter of a Lyons' weaver, didn't she? That is the truth, and I'm not ashamed of it. She also told you that I didn't love my first husband, and that I deceived him, I suppose. The fact is, he never did inspire me with any other feeling than gratitude, but he asked nothing more, and he never had any reason to complain of me."

"Mademoiselle Blanche pretended that he poisoned himself."

"I scorn to notice that calumny. It is as unworthy of notice as she is. Fortunately, I shall never be obliged to hear her name mentioned again."

"Who knows?" said Puymirol. "She let me understand that she had some powerful weapons against you—letters."

"Letters! Why, didn't I tell you just now that I had never written to anyone but Pierre in my life?"

"That would be quite enough. A few lines suffice to compromise one at times, and if Dargental was ever foolish enough to show a note of yours to that girl, she may have managed to obtain possession of it."

The countess turned pale, and her assurance failed her. "I will never believe that," she said, in a voice that trembled in spite of all her efforts. "Pierre treated me badly at one time, but he was incapable of intrusting any damaging secret to this creature; besides, she wouldn't have kept it. I authorize you to tell her, from me, that what she says is false, and that I'm not afraid of her."

"Nothing would suit me better but I don't visit her, and there is very little probability of my meeting her anywhere."

Madame de Lescombat reflected for a moment, and then said: "But what if I asked you to see her again? What if I begged of you to question her, and discover what she referred to when she threatened to produce I don't know what proofs against me?"

"I should comply with your request, of course; but if Blanche suspected that I came on your behalf, she would probably be emboldened, and might publish your letters if she has any."

"She hasn't any," was the quick response, "but you are right. It is best to let the matter drop, and not to trouble ourselves any further about this creature."

Puymirol was satisfied. The countess had fallen into the trap set for her. The anxiety she had failed to conceal conclusively proved how much importance she attached to the recovery of some particular letter, and this letter was unquestionably one of those contained in the pocketbook.

However, before Puymirol could decide what use he should make of the advantage thus gained, his companion said, thoughtfully: "It is strange, but I talk to you exactly as I should talk to an intimate friend. It is true that I am much better acquainted with you than you suppose, for although Pierre seldom brought you to see me he was always talking about you."

"He was not particularly enthusiastic in his praises, I suppose?" interrupted Adhémar, smiling.

"Nor in his censure. He was inclined to be jealous of you; but he liked you, and could not refrain from doing justice to your qualities. He used to say that you were always brave, and that you never despaired, either at the card-table or in your love affairs. It was the same with him; and it was for that very reason that I loved him, though my love for him certainly cost me dear. Yes, why should I hide from you the fact that I have lent him large amounts over and over again. Still, I never even regretted the inroads that his passion for gambling made in my fortune. I was only too happy to help him, and I think I should almost have hated him if he had refused my proffered aid."

"You are presenting Dargental to me in a new light," said Puymirol, biting his lips.

"Oh, I see that you have your prejudices like all the rest of your sex. You think it perfectly right and natural to deceive a woman and reduce her to despair by deserting her, and yet your pride revolts at the mere thought of accepting a pecuniary favour from her. Well, for myself, I don't dislike the idea that my lover should treat me as an equal. Dargental, at first, had the same ideas as you have, but I succeeded in winning him over to my way of thinking; and if I ever pledge myself to another man, I shall require him to sacrifice the foolish pride you seem to admire so much."

"You would have great difficulty in converting me. I would rather resign you than submit."

"You are not my lover. If you were, I flatter myself that I should succeed in overcoming your opposition. I should say to you, 'You lost ten thousand francs last night, on parole, and you are miserable because you don't know how you will manage to pay the money. Here it is. Take it, or I shall know that you do not love me.'"

Adhémar started. He, himself, had lost exactly ten thousand francs on the evening before, and Madame de Lescombat's shot told. Was the remark really intended for him, or was it by a mere chance that she mentioned such a case, and that exact amount? He did not know, but however that might be, he must make some reply. "That is a test to which I should not like to be subjected," he exclaimed. "It would be a cruel alternative, you must admit."

"Perhaps so; but come, Fortune has frowned upon you. You admit it, do you not?"

"Well, I do admit it. For a fortnight past, I have done nothing but lose. One would think that Dargental's death had brought me bad luck."

"It will bring misfortune upon others as well. Your last evening at baccarat was most disastrous, was it not?"

"How do you know?"

"Why, there was a member of your club in the tribune at the horse show, and on seeing you bow to me he naturally spoke of you, and of the game you played last evening. He told me that you w re an excellent player, as cool when you lost as when you won. That is all very well; but one must be able to pay one's debts of honour."

"I shall pay mine," said Adhémar drily.

"I have wounded you, I see," replied the countess. "Believe me, the offence was unintentional. I have a bad habit of not concealing my feelings, and of imagining that I have a right to oblige those I like. I heard that you were embarrassed pecuniarily, and my first impulse was to help you. It was for that reason that I asked you to call here. If you refuse my offer you will wound me deeply, I assure you."

"What would you think of me if I accepted it?"

"I should think that I inspired you with sufficient liking and confidence to make you willing to become my debtor. I merely propose a loan. With Pierre, it was different. Pierre was to marry me. We had the same interests, and my fortune was his; but I shall accommodate you exactly as one friend accommodates another, and if you insist upon it, I am willing to accept your note for the amount."

"My note would not be worth more than a verbal promise, for I have no security to give, and I should probably be unable to meet the note when it fell due. If I consented to accept your offer, I should never dare to set foot here again, and that would be a terrible deprivation for me."

"You wish to see me again, you say, and yet you hesitate to make this slight sacrifice of pride? It is not in this way that I wish to be loved."

"Then you would be willing to accept my love and devotion?" exclaimed Puymirol.

"A coquette might give you an evasive answer. But I am made of different stuff, and I frankly answer 'Yes.'"

Acting upon the impulse of the moment, Adhémar made a movement as if to throw himself at the countess's feet, but she checked him with a gesture, and said, smiling: "I desire no rash or premature protestations. Listen to me before you go any further. I have been sufficiently frank with you for you to believe me when I tell you what I think, and feel. At my age a woman can hardly resign herself to perpetual widowhood, and for that reason I was on the point of marrying Pierre, though I might have done much better, for I had serious reason to complain of him. But you are not going to ask me to marry you, or even to engage myself to you forthwith, I suppose?"

"No, for you would refuse."

"No doubt; and, besides, the man who cares to win me must be my friend and my ally against my enemies."

"Is it possible that you have any enemies?"

"Have you forgotten Blanche Pornic? She might injure me greatly; and I cannot contend unaided against a woman who has nothing to lose."

Puymirol now began to understand the countess's advances, and his self-possession returned to him, in a measure. It was evident that she wished to bind him to her at any cost.

"You may be right," he said, after a moment's silence. "Blanche is capable of anything; besides, she has good reason to feel anxious, for the authorities believe that Dargental died by violence, and she has been closely questioned, and may be examined again."

"Can she be accused of murdering him?"

"Not exactly, as she is still at large. But the police are looking for the murderer; and rumour attributes the crime to one of our friend's former sweethearts, who hired some one to kill him, so as to regain possession of certain letters."

"What did I tell you a moment ago? This creature undoubtedly wrote him something that revealed her in her true character. I am sure of it; for Pierre told me one day that he had something in his possession which would suffice to send her to the Assizes. I am perfectly willing to repeat that to the magistrate."

"That would be very imprudent; for Mademoiselle Pornic, in self-defence, might declare that you also had written to Pierre, and that you were even more interested than she was in regaining possession of your correspondence. At the beginning of our conversation, you yourself admitted that there were some danger in this."

"And I asked you to try and frighten Mademoiselle Pornic out of the notion of slandering me. You politely refused. I shall, perhaps, be obliged to apply to a bolder person. Where does this woman live?"

"At No. 34, Avenue de Messine. But it would be useless for you to apply to her. Not a single letter was found at Dargental's. Besides, his pocket-book had been stolen from him."

"A Russia-leather pocket-book, with his initial and a marquis's coronet upon it!" exclaimed the countess, greatly agitated. "I gave it to him."

"Well, the question is to ascertain into whose hands it has fallen," remarked Puymirol. "If it has come into Blanche Pornic's possession, she will have destroyed her own letters, and have preserved yours."

"I can compel her to return them to me."

"I doubt it. If I thought it possible, I should not hesitate to make the attempt."

"My hand and fortune shall be the reward of the man who will restore my letters to me," said the countess, boldly.

It was impossible to declare more plainly that she was at the mercy of the person who had possession of her missives to Dargental, and Puymirol, still under the charm of her wonderful beauty, felt anxious to win the promised reward. "I will do all in my power to serve you," he said, rising, after he had pressed a kiss upon her soft white hand.

"Then begin by taking the five hundred louis you need to pay your gambling debts," was the quick reply.

"Anything but that," rejoined Puymirol, firmly. "Will you permit me to call again to-morrow?"

"At any hour you like. I shall always be at home to you."

Puymirol certainly deserved some credit for refusing Madame de Lescombat's offers of pecuniary assistance, for never since the outset of his struggles in Parisian waters had he found himself in an equally trying position. A fortnight's continuous ill luck had reduced him to penury. It is true that he still had twenty-four hours' respite left him, but if he had had a month at his disposal, he would have been no better off, for he had nothing to expect from any one. George Caumont could render him no assistance, and his Aunt Bessèges would not send him a penny, even had he merely asked her to advance him a portion of his next quarter's allowance.

There is nothing really better than violent exercise for dispelling gloomy thoughts, and, being fully aware of this fact, Puymirol, after taking leave of the countess, repaired to his club, and entered the fencing-room, in the hope of finding some pleasant company, and of gaining an appetite by a bout with some foemen worthy of his steel. He fenced in turn with three of the best swordsmen present, even worsted the professor, and then having attained a tranquil state of mind, he began to consider where he should dine, and in what way he should spend his evening.

The club dinner not being quite ready, he decided to patronise the Lion d'Or, where he had not set foot since the catastrophe. He strolled there and went in without noticing a gentleman who was talking with the doorkeeper, and who entered immediately behind him. However, the first person he saw inside was Blanche Pornic, seated at table with a young and handsome officer. The meeting displeased him, but it was too late to beat a retreat. Blanche would think he was purposely avoiding her, and he did not wish to arouse her suspicions. She gave him a friendly smile as he passed by—a smile which made her companion turn to look at the new comer who was greeted so familiarly. Puymirol responded by touching his hat politely, and then walked on to the other end of the room, for he felt that the right moment for an interview with Blanche had not yet arrived, and he did not care to be in her immediate neighbourhood. Having ensconced himself in a corner, he ordered a first-rate dinner, and under the influence of some generous wine his ideas soon assumed a roseate hue. It was only when he had finished his dessert and had just poured himself out a little old brandy, that he noticed that a person dining in front of him—the gentleman who had followed him into the restaurant—was staring at him with strange persistency. Puymirol returned the stare with interest, and perceived that this stranger was a man considerably older than himself, carefully dressed, but with somewhat the look of a provincial. He did not once lower his eyes, but kept them persistently riveted on Puymirol, and the latter, who was by no means patient, soon called a waiter and ordered him in a loud voice to go and ask that gentleman why he was staring at him in such an extraordinary manner. The frightened servant did not seem at all anxious to deliver this disagreeable message, but the offender had heard the order, and laying his napkin on the table, he quietly rose, and came straight towards Puymirol, who prepared himself for an attack. However, the stranger, probably in order to convince Adhémar that he had no hostile intentions, began by bowing very politely, and then said, in a conciliatory tone: "Excuse me, sir, for having looked at you in an offensive manner. But I was trying to find some excuse for speaking to you, and now that you have furnished it, I will ask the favour of a moment's conversation."

"What have you to say to me?" retorted Puymirol, without abandoning his threatening attitude.

"Permit me first to take a seat at your table. If I continue to talk to you standing, I shall attract the attention of all the people present. They are already beginning to watch us, and they will think I am trying to pick a quarrel with you, whereas my intentions are really of the most peaceable kind. Besides, what I have to say to you is strictly confidential."

"Very well, take a seat and explain yourself, but be brief. First of all, who are you?"

"My name would have no significance to you," said the stranger, sitting down. "I don't know yours, nor do I wish to know it."

"But how can you have any business with me if you don't know my name? You are fooling me, and I am going—"

"Pray, grant me a hearing. I was at the door of the restaurant when you came in, and I asked the door-porter if you had not come here one day, under circumstances which he was bound to remember. He replied in the affirmative, so I followed you in, wondering how I should manage to enter into conversation with you. Pray, believe that I should not have watched for your coming here during a whole fortnight, if mere idle curiosity had prompted my desire to make your acquaintance."

"You dare to admit that you have been playing the spy on me for a fortnight?"

"I was not playing the spy, I merely told the doorkeeper that I would give him two louis if he would point out to me a gentleman who came here one morning in a cab to lunch with a party in a private room. He was anxious to secure the promised reward, of course, but you did not make your appearance until to-night."

"Well, confine yourself to facts. What do you want with me?"

"Before explaining myself more fully, I wish to satisfy myself that I am not making a mistake. So allow me, sir, to ask you one question, only one. Did you not, on Wednesday, the 9th of April, pass through the Place du Carrousel in a cab which turned into the Rue de Rivoli?"

"I have passed through the Place du Carrousel hundreds of times in my life," said Adhémar, "but I am not at all sure that I passed through it on the day you mention. I have no reason to recollect such an insignificant occurrence."

"You came here to lunch with some friends. You were not alone in the cab—"

"Well, say there were two of us, but what difference can that make to you and why have you taken so much trouble to look me up?"

"It did, indeed, cost me a deal of trouble. My only clue was the number of the cab, so I first tried to find the driver and ultimately succeeded. He remembered you very well on account of the liberal gratuity you gave him on dismissing him, and he told me he had set you and your friend down outside the Lion d'Or. I then spoke to the door-porter of the restaurant, who said that he knew you by sight, but that he was unable to give me your name or address; and the head waiter either could not or would not tell me anything. I again applied to the door-porter, giving him two louis, and promising him two more. He knew that you dined here sometimes, and he promised to point you out to me the first time you came if I had patience enough to wait for you every day between seven and eight. I accepted his offer, and by waiting patiently, I have at last accomplished my object."

"Well, well, come to the facts, for although you have been talking ten minutes or more, we have made no progress whatever." Puymirol had now abandoned all idea of repulsing the stranger. His curiosity was greatly excited, and he determined not to part with this man until he had subjected him to a close examination.

"I am coming to the facts, sir, and I trust you will not take offence at the question I am going to ask you. Did you find a pocket-book in the cab which brought you here a fortnight ago?"

"Here it comes at last!" thought Puymirol. "I have you now, my fine fellow."

"A pocket-book?" he repeated aloud in pretended astonishment. "No, certainly not. Had there been one in the cab I should of course have left it there, and as you know the number of the vehicle you should apply to the authorities, or rather to the driver, as you have succeeded in finding him."

"The driver saw nothing of it. He told me so, and I am sure that he told the truth."

"Then you may as well abandon all hope of recovering your pocket-book. It must have been appropriated by one of the persons who hired the vehicle afterwards. Did it contain any bank-notes?"

"Not one; nothing, in fact, but a few lottery tickets which amount to nothing, for no one ever wins anything in the gigantic humbugs that are so extensively advertised."

"Then, why do you attach so much importance to the recovery of such worthless property?"

The stranger reflected for a moment, and then said, gravely: "I don't know who you are, sir, but I feel sure that you are an honourable man, so I do not hesitate to tell you that a woman's reputation is at stake. The pocket-book also contained several letters."

"Good! I understand now. You fear that these letters may have fallen into the hands of some person who will make a bad use of them. That is improbable, however, as they could hardly interest the finder. But how the deuce did you happen to leave them in the cab—for I suppose they were addressed to you?"

"You are mistaken, sir. The woman who wrote them commissioned me to claim them from the man who received them. I was fortunate enough to obtain possession of them, but only after a deal of difficulty. I will even admit to you that I was obliged to threaten the scoundrel who held them, and who intended to make use of them. He finally yielded, but he hoped to regain possession of them, and with that object he had me followed by two of his hirelings. I found that out, and surmised that his spies first intended to find out where I was going, then to spring upon me just as I was entering the house, and wrest the pocket-book from me."

"In broad daylight, and in the heart of Paris? Why, you need only have summoned a policeman or some passer-by to foil the scoundrels."

"That was exactly what they wanted. Had I called for assistance, my assailants would have accused me of stealing the pocket-book. A crowd would have gathered round us, and we should have been taken before a commissary of police, who would have found the pocket-book upon me. An examination of its contents would have been enough, and more than enough, to ruin the person I wished to save."

"Well, if I had been in your place, I should have crossed the bridge, and thrown the pocket-book into the Seine."

"Yes, I might have done that, but the idea did not occur to me. I was just turning out of the Rue de Rivoli when I saw several cabs waiting to enter that street. On passing the last one I laid my hand on the ledge of the open window, and dropped the pocket-book inside."

"The men who were following you must have see your gesture."

"The fact that they continued to follow me is sufficient proof to the contrary. I amused myself by leading them as far as Montrouge. There I entered a house that has two doors, and succeeded in escaping from them."

"But you must have expected that the occupants of the cab would pick up the pocket-book."

"Yes; but as it could not be of the slightest use to them, I hoped I should regain possession of it. I took good care to note the number of the cab, and you see I accomplished my object, as I have succeeded in finding you."

"That is to say, you suppose I am one of the persons who were in the cab at the time."

"I am sure of it, and I am also sure that, touched by the trying situation in which I am placed, you will return the pocket-book to me."

"You are too hasty in your conclusions, for even if the article were in my possession, I should not return it without due consideration. In the first place, I should have to know whom I have to deal with, for there is nothing to prove that you are not an emissary of the man, who, as you pretend, hired some fellows to follow you. You would have to tell me your name and address, in order that I might make the necessary inquiries respecting you."

"My name and address are a secret that I am not free to divulge. Be more generous. Restore me the letters without demanding my name. It would be a most kind and noble action, and later on, I shall be able to repay the debt of gratitude I owe you." Puymirol seemed in no haste to reply. He now felt sure that Dargental's murderer sat before him, and he was asking himself what course he had better pursue. "I can now confess that I fully expected to purchase the pocket-book from the finder," continued the stranger. "I was ready and willing to give him as many thousand francs as he chose to ask for it; but, on seeing you, I realised that such a course was out of the question. One can not offer money to a gentleman like you. One can only appeal to his feelings, and invoke his pity for an imprudent woman."

"You argue exactly as if I had the letters in my pocket," said Adhémar, in order to gain time.

"In your pocket, or in your desk at home, which amounts to the same thing, as it is in your power to restore them to me in either case."

"You would consent to accompany me home, then?"

"Instantly, if you wish it."

"But I don't wish it. You refuse to tell me where you live, so I don't see why I should tell you where I live."

"Well, there is nothing to prevent you from making an appointment with me for to-morrow at this same restaurant."

"I only make appointments with my friends."

"Am I to take this as your final answer?"

"Yes, and I will now state my reasons. I did see this pocket-book. It fell into my lap. Now that you have enlightened me, there is no reason why I should deny the fact any longer. But, as for returning the article, it is impossible, as it is no longer in my possession."

"You can at least tell me what you have done with it."

"I did what any one else would have done with it. I left it at the office of the commissary of police."

The stranger turned perceptibly paler, but he did not lose countenance. "At the office of the commissary of the Chaussée d'Antin district?" he asked.

"Do you think of claiming the article?" rejoined Puymirol, wishing to evade this rather embarrassing question.

"Possibly. Before doing so, however, I must consult the person who is most interested in the matter. But you, no doubt, opened the pocket-book before taking it to the commissary's office?"

"Yes; and on discovering that it only contained some papers, my first impulse was to throw it out of the window, but on reflection I said to myself: Russian leather has its value, and I thought that the papers might furnish a clue to the owner of the article."

"Did you read the letters?"

"I glanced at them, and seeing that they bore no signature I replaced them in the pocket-book," replied Puymirol, at the same time suddenly noticing the direction of the stranger's glance, which was turned upon his—Puymirol's chest. Instinctively raising his hand he found that one end of the pocket-book was now projecting from his breast-pocket. He had unbuttoned his coat on sitting down to dinner, but he now hastily closed it again.

"I am greatly obliged to you," said the stranger, slowly. "For I now know where the letters are. I am very sorry to have troubled you, and I will not inflict my company upon you any longer." With these words he rose, returned to his table, and asked the waiter for his bill.

"I see your little game," thought Puymirol, "you intend to follow me when I leave the restaurant. Try it, old fellow, we shall see." And then, wishing to be quite free in his movements, he also asked for his score.

The two bills were brought at the same time. They both paid, and the stranger rose to go. While he was putting on his overcoat, however, Puymirol asked in a loud voice for some cigars of a particular brand, which, as he knew perfectly well, was not kept in the house. This was done solely for the purpose of convincing the stranger that he did not intend to leave the table for several minutes, and the fellow fell into the trap. Puymirol saw him pass down the main staircase, and disappear behind the curtains of the vestibule. A moment afterwards, he also rose, slipped on his overcoat, and passed out, not by the main exit, but by a side-door, communicating with the Hôtel du Helder, of which the restaurant is an adjunct. He duly proceeded to the hotel entrance, and, peering out, looked up and down the street. It was dark, and no foot passengers were visible, but, finally, inside a wine-shop, brilliantly lighted up and only a few yards off, he saw a person standing near the glass door with his eyes fixed on the restaurant. Puymirol waited ten minutes or more watching this man, and at last the glass door opened, and the fellow crossed the street to the Lion d'Or and spoke to the doorkeeper, who at once darted up the stairs leading to the restaurant. "Good!" thought Puymirol, "the scoundrel wants to find out if I am still at table. When he finds that I have left he will decamp without loss of time. I hope the head-waiter won't tell him which way I went out. But if he does, this man will never suspect that I am still here, and if he should come this way, I can easily conceal myself."

A moment later, the doorkeeper returned and evidently reported the result of his mission. The stranger slipped a gratuity into his hand, crossed the street, and then walked slowly towards the Boulevard Haussmann, without pausing to look around or behind, as he would have done had he suspected that anyone meant to follow him. "My ruse has succeeded," muttered Puymirol, "and the rascal can't escape me now. I certainly mean to follow him, and when I have found out where he lives, all the rest will be plain sailing."

On reaching the end of the Rue du Helder, the man paused for an instant, and then turned down the Rue Taitbout. "Perhaps he isn't going straight home," thought Puymirol. "When he threw the pocket-book into the cab he was bound for the left bank of the river, so he must live in that direction. Perhaps he is now going to see the woman whose cause he has espoused. I must be careful."

Puymirol did not at first realize that to follow a man successfully the pursuer must remain some little distance behind. If he follows him too closely, he is almost sure to attract his attention, and this almost happened at the corner of the Rue de Provence, when the stranger was obliged to stop short to let a carriage pass. He went on his way almost immediately, but it was a lesson that Puymirol profited by. The stranger now went up the Rue de la Chaussée d'Antin, as far as the Place de la Trinité, where he again hesitated, and Puymirol had to hastily conceal himself behind a vehicle. However, the stranger finally decided to cross the square and went down the Rue de Londres, but on reaching the Place de l'Europe he stopped again. A train was passing under the railway bridge, and he leant over the railing to watch it. One might have fancied that he had nothing better to do than to kill time by strolling about the streets. At, last, however, he leisurely turned into the Rue de Madrid, and it suddenly occurred to Puymirol that this street crossed the Avenue de Messine, where Blanche Pornic resided. True, he had seen Blanche with an officer at the restaurant, but she might have finished her dinner and have returned home in a cab before now, so possibly this man, who had murdered Dargental, was her hireling. But on reaching the corner of the Avenue de Messine, the stranger, instead of entering that thoroughfare, walked on as far as the Rue de Vigny, a short street, at the end of which the Lescombat mansion stands. The mystery was solved. The stranger was certainly going to the countess's house. He was not in Blanche's employ but in hers. Puymirol forthwith returned to his first plan, which was to make a direct attack upon Madame de Lescombat. He now held her secret, and she could not refuse him anything, for she was at his mercy. Still, it was necessary for him to make sure that the man entered her house, and for some minutes past the pursuit had been attended with much more difficulty. This part of Paris is but little frequented in the evening, and Puymirol and the man he was following were the only persons in the street, so that, if the stranger turned, he could hardly fail to notice his pursuer. However, the stranger did not turn. On the contrary, he walked on with his head bowed upon his breast, and a cigar in his mouth, apparently oblivious to everything transpiring around him. He was already passing the high wall that inclosed the grounds of the Lescombat mansion. There was here a small gate, but, instead of ringing at it, he pushed on towards the boulevard, where the main entrance was situated, and Puymirol finally saw him disappear round the corner. He followed on in hot haste. Two windows of Madame de Lescombat's abode were lighted up—those of the boudoir where the countess usually sat—but the stranger was not in front of the gate. Puymirol thought he must have already gone in, and he himself was about to ring, when he perceived the fellow standing in the middle of the thoroughfare, and gazing at a fountain. However, the light of an approaching omnibus was visible in the distance, and Puymirol thought that the stranger might be waiting for it. But he was again mistaken. The omnibus passed on; the man crossed the boulevard, and turning into the next street, walked off in an exactly opposite direction to that taken by the omnibus. "No matter," muttered Puymirol, "I will not lose sight of him until I see him enter a house. Even then, I must satisfy myself before I leave, that the house he enters is really the one he lives in. Baccarat has nearly ruined me, but I still have enough money about me to bribe a doorkeeper. At all events, I shall persevere until the end."

After going a short distance, the man turned suddenly to the right, into a street that Puymirol was not acquainted with, but which must lead back to the point they had left a few moments before. "Can he have noticed me, and is he trying to throw me off the scent?" Puymirol asked himself for the first time. "Or, has he allowed me to follow him, in order to draw me into some trap? It would not astonish me on the part of such a scoundrel as he is." Indeed, the fellow knew that the pocket-book was in Puymirol's possession, for he had seen it projecting from his coat at the restaurant, and he had every reason to suppose that the letters were still inside it. This reflection made Adhémar pause, but only for a moment. He had gone too far to retreat, so he hurried on again, soliloquising: "Fortunately, I left the letters with George. There are only some lottery tickets in the case, and, after all, I don't see why I should even leave them inside." And, thereupon, he opened the pocket-book, took out the tickets and slipped them into his waistcoat pocket, replacing the case in his coat.

The stranger was now some distance in advance, for the person walking along so rapidly about half-way up the street must certainly be he, and Puymirol, seeing him again turn to the right, hastened on regardless of the noise his boots made on the asphalt. But he had mistaken another pedestrian for the enemy he wished to overtake, for just as he was least expecting it, his foe, emerging from an alley in which he had concealed himself, sprung out upon him, and seized him by the throat. Puymirol was strong, but the attack was so sudden and so violent, that he had not time to defend himself. He felt a violent twist, and that was all. His breath failed him, his arms fluttered, and he lost his footing, falling, half-fainting, upon the pavement. He did not entirely lose consciousness, but his sensations were vague and confused. He fancied that there was a heavy weight upon his chest, that his coat was being unbuttoned and his pockets searched, but all this was done so quickly that he was scarcely aware of it. How many minutes elapsed before he fully regained his senses, he never knew; but when he did recover them, he perceived that his assailant had disappeared. He rose with difficulty, and while satisfying himself that he had no bones broken, he likewise discovered that his pocket-book had disappeared. His watch, his money, and the lottery tickets were safe, however. His assailant had merely wanted to get the letters, and he was foiled in his attempt, for he had not found them.

Puymirol endeavoured to console himself with this reflection, but although he still possessed the letters he did not know what use to make of them. Nothing short of a miracle was now required to extricate him from his dilemma, but Puymirol was no believer in miracles.

## III.

WHILE Puymirol was engaged in these adventures, George Caumont was dreaming of his love. He had gone to the club after dinner in the hope of finding his friend, but failing in this, he had comforted himself with the thought that Puymirol would be sure to return home sooner or later, and accordingly he went back to the Rue de Medicis where they occupied separate suites of apartments in the same house. George fell asleep dreaming of Gabrielle Verdon; but as soon as he awoke in the morning, he repaired to his friend's rooms of which he had a key, just as Adhémar had a key to his, and on going in, he found the bed undisturbed. This discovery made him rather anxious, and after waiting in vain all the morning, George finally determined to go in search of Adhémar. He first repaired to the residence of the Countess de Lescombat, knowing that Puymirol had gone there, but a fresh disappointment awaited him, for the countess was out, and the doorkeeper, whilst admitting that M. de Puymirol had called on the day before, added that he had only remained a short time. George thereupon left his card, with the announcement that he would call upon Madame de Lescombat on the following afternoon, and re-entering his cab, was driven to the club. He learned that his friend had been fencing there on the day before, but that nothing had been seen of him since then; whereupon he made a tour of various gambling-houses, where Puymirol might have spent the night, but no one could give him any news. Disheartened by this failure, George finally drove back to the Rue de Medicis with a vague hope of finding that Adhémar had returned. But in this expectation he was likewise disappointed, and after writing a few lines, in which he begged Puymirol to wait for him in case he came back before he did, he made a hasty toilet and repaired to the Luxembourg garden in search of Gabrielle and her mother. He soon found them seated alone near a clump of shrubbery, Madame Verdon reading a newspaper, whilst Gabrielle was busy with some crotchet work. M. Rochas was not with them, though there were three chairs. George realised that they were expecting him, and that Gabrielle had chosen this spot so that they might not be disturbed. She gave a cry of delight on perceiving him, and her mother greeted him with an encouraging smile.

"Your coming is most opportune, sir," she graciously remarked. "We were just speaking of you. Yes; I was just saying to Gabrielle that her brother is very unlike you. You are faithful to your friends, whereas that naughty boy ignores me entirely. Would you believe it, we have not seen him since the horse show, and he reached Paris only yesterday morning. He will make his appearance sooner or later, I suppose, and consider himself deeply aggrieved if we do not give him a cordial reception. But, let us say no more about that, but talk of something else. My daughter has told me everything."

George bowed, but remained silent.

"Come, don't be over modest," continued Madame Verdon. "You have known ever since yesterday that Gabrielle loves you, and that I approve of her choice. She has never concealed anything from me, and she has repeated to me every word that passed between you. It is as well you should know that I have always told her: 'My dear girl, marry to suit yourself. I shall have nothing to do with the affair, excepting as regards giving my consent when you ask me for it. I think you incapable of loving a man unworthy of you. I shall, therefore, trust to your discernment, and take care not to thwart your inclinations.'"

This little speech rather surprised George, but he was obliged to admit that there was considerable good sense in the lady's theories, and he was really grateful to her for thus breaking the ice. Besides, he could not forget that Gabrielle's frankness, far from shocking, had delighted him, and he could not consistently blame the mother for acting in the same way.

Madame Verdon added some remarks as to George's father, his own position and prospects, and finally exclaimed: "I feel sure that you will make my daughter happy, and as it does not seem necessary to consult her—"

"Not at all necessary, mamma. I am already engaged," exclaimed Gabrielle, gaily.

"Then," resumed Madame Verdon, "I give my consent. And now, my dear son-in-law, you can confer with my notary whenever you please. He will explain my daughter's financial situation to you, and you can explain yours to him. Gabrielle's fortune is entirely at her own disposal. She has her share of her father's property, and I shall also give her a dowry of two hundred thousand francs. Your father will certainly do something on his side, so you will be able to begin housekeeping with at least thirty thousand francs a year."

"You are too generous," murmured George. "I wish mademoiselle were poor. In that case, she could not doubt my disinterestedness."

"Do you think that I doubt it now?" asked Gabrielle, quickly.

"I am sure that I don't," chimed in Madame Verdon, "and as you love each other, that is enough. Everything else is of little moment, I have always been of that opinion, and when I was young nothing could have induced me to marry for money, nor could anything induce me to do such a thing even now." George pricked up his ears. He realised that the lady's confession would not be much longer deferred. "The moment has come," she continued, "to inform you of a project, which my daughter has, perhaps, mentioned to you. I am about to marry again, and I am sure you will approve of my resolve, when you become better acquainted with my intended husband, whom I introduced to you yesterday at the Palais de l'Industrie. Monsieur Jacques Rochas is several years older than myself, but I should not care to marry a young man. He is a widower, but he has no children, and he is wealthy. His disposition and character suit me. I am perfectly well aware that this is no reason why they should please every one, and I shall not insist upon my daughter and my son-in-law living with us. My plans for the future are made. Jacques and I intend to travel a good deal, and when we settle down, we shall purchase a château not far from Paris, where we can entertain our friends. You will always be very welcome there, you and Gabrielle, but as neither of you has much liking for a country life, you had better install yourselves comfortably inside Paris. Remember that I shall never cease to take an interest in my dear Gabrielle's welfare and in yours. I even hope to contribute to your happiness. I was anxious to tell you all this, for I did not wish you to engage yourself to my daughter without a full knowledge of all the circumstances. If this explicit statement of my intentions does not displease you, it will only remain for us to fix the wedding-day."

"The earlier the date, the better pleased I shall be," said George, with an ardent glance at Mademoiselle Verdon.

"Well, I can not speak for Gabrielle, who maintains a determined silence, but I should like to leave France for Switzerland—Monsieur Rochas's birthplace—about the middle of May."

"A fortnight would be ample time to accomplish all the formalities."

"Let us say a fortnight, then. I will leave it to you young people to fix the precise day; still I shall forthwith announce this great event to Monsieur Rochas, who will feel very glad I'm sure; and that young rogue, Albert, will condescend, I hope, to lead his sister to the altar."

"Are you not afraid that your son may be displeased at not being consulted?" inquired George.

"My son has no voice in the matter."

"And he loves me too well not to rejoice at my happiness," added Gabrielle, quickly. "He will be our best friend."

"Well, if he goes on as he has begun, you are not likely to see much of him," said Madame Verdon, gaily. "But how about your friend, Monsieur de Puymirol? I hope he will act as your best man, or at least as one of your witnesses on your marriage-day. He is a very handsome young fellow, and as you two are inseparable, I hear, I hope you will soon introduce him to us."

"Certainly," murmured George. "I haven't seen him to-day, but I shall meet him this evening, no doubt, and—"

"Oh, I can very readily understand why you did not bring him with you, this morning," interrupted Madame Verdon. "On such an occasion the most intimate friends are in the way. But, speaking of intimate friends, I must tell you that there is a person whom you will see a great deal of when Gabrielle becomes your wife, for he cannot bear her out of his sight. That is our worthy friend, Roch Plancoët."

George gave the ladies a questioning look as if asking what was the nature of the bond that united this stranger to Mademoiselle Verdon. "Roch was my father's foster-brother," said Gabrielle, prompted, probably, by a desire to reassure her lover. "They were brought up together, and after my father's death, he could not make up his mind to abandon my brother and myself, for he had been deeply attached to us from our infancy. When we came to Paris, he came here as well. He is a most devoted friend, but he is painfully shy. You have never yet seen him, and never will see him, in my mother's drawing-room, but not a day passes without his coming to the house to spend an hour or two with me, and he would go through fire and water to spare me pain. He is old enough to be my father, and he loves me as if I were really his daughter."

"Yes, you are a great favourite with him," said Madame Verdon, "but every one is not fortunate enough to be in his good graces. He is very fond of your brother, too, but he is not at all partial to me, and I am quite sure that he does not like Monsieur Rochas. By the way, Gabrielle, I am surprised that we have seen nothing of him since yesterday morning—"

"So I have found you at last," at this moment cried a clear, ringing voice that made all three of the party glance up hastily. "I have been looking for you fully three quarters of an hour. I met Roch at your door, and he told me you must be here."

"Albert!" exclaimed the young girl, springing up and flinging her arms about the neck of her brother, who embraced her heartily in return. "We have been so uneasy about you!" she cried. "Where have you been, you bad fellow?"

"Oh, I had to dine with some comrades, of course. It would not be worth while winning a prize, if one didn't celebrate one's good fortune by a dinner afterwards."

"Nonsense!" exclaimed Madame Verdon. "Confess that you have been dancing attendance upon the damsel who threw you some violets."

"I haven't the slightest idea what you mean, mamma," replied the young lieutenant, frowning.

"Oh, well, we will say no more about it," rejoined Madame Verdon. "You are no longer a schoolboy, and I have no right to keep you tied to my apron strings, but if I were your colonel, I should put you under arrest. But I have two pieces of news for you. First, however, allow me to introduce Monsieur George Caumont, who will soon be your brother-in-law. We were just deciding upon the wedding-day."

Albert instantly became serious, but a questioning glance which he gave Gabrielle elicited from her a happy smile. "Do you remember what I wrote to you last winter?" she asked. "It is true I did not mention any names, but—"

"I should think I did remember!" exclaimed the young officer, "and I was going to inquire about the happy man this very day. As it is this gentleman, I must ask him to shake hands with me. I trust we shall be good friends."

"I sincerely hope so," replied George, cordially shaking the lieutenant's proffered hand.

"You don't belong to the army?" resumed Albert.

"No, indeed," exclaimed Madame Verdon. "Monsieur Caumont is just completing his law studies. His father is a landed proprietor in Normandy."

"Well, Monsieur Caumont pleases Gabrielle, and that is enough for me, mamma. If he didn't, I would not take him for a brother-in-law."

"My preference has always been for marriages of inclination," replied Madame Verdon; "love matches, if you like—and you will need no better proof of that than my announcement of my own approaching marriage with Monsieur Jacques Rochas." Albert turned pale, but did not say a word. It was evident that he was making a violent effort to control himself. "Monsieur Rochas was your guardian," continued Madame Verdon, drily, "and for ten years he has been almost one of the family. Our marriage is a settled thing, and nothing that you can say, will make any difference. However, Gabrielle's wedding is the first thing to be considered. I expect it will take place in about a fortnight's time."

"And yours, mother?" asked Albert.

"Mine will come off next month, in Switzerland, probably. On my return to France, I shall live in the country, and very quietly."

"That will be best," remarked Albert, gravely.

George began to look very uncomfortable, and Gabrielle had tears in her eyes. "I am sorry to leave you, my dear Monsieur Caumont," now said the mother, "but it is growing chilly, and my daughter and I must return home. Remember, however, that from this time forth our home is yours. I leave you with my son, whom you ought to convert to a sensible way of thinking."

Madame Verdon rose up as she spoke, and Gabrielle followed her, but not until she had given her brother and her lover a meaning glance. The two young fellows, on being left alone, strolled towards a café at Albert's suggestion, and while quaffing a glass of beer, they began to chat like two old friends. Albert, who showed himself remarkably communicative, related his adventures with Mademoiselle Blanche Pornic, beginning with the horse-show and winding up with the announcement that he had dined with her on the previous evening at the Lion d'Or.

"At the Lion d'Or! that's singular," muttered Georgo, thinking of the lunch ordered by Dargental, and at which Blanche had figured so prominently.

"Why is it singular? It seems to be a very popular restaurant. We had scarcely sat down when in came a gentleman whom Blanche knew, and whose name she told me—a Monsieur de Puymirol."

"Puymirol! are you sure that you are not mistaken in the name?" cried George. This was the first news that he had received of his friend for twenty-four hours, and it seemed strange that tidings should reach him in such a roundabout way.

"Perfectly sure, for Blanche told me an interesting story in connection with this gentleman. He was the intimate friend, it seems, of a Monsieur Dargental who was murdered a fortnight or so ago."

"Did she tell you that?"

"Yes, and a deal more. She pretends to think that the gentleman in question was murdered by one of his old flames—a Countess de Lescombat, whom she seems to hate. I even suspect that they must once have been rivals. But is this story really true? I never saw anything about it in the newspapers."

"There is this much truth in it: Dargental was killed by a pistol shot, but no one knows who fired it."

"I certainly hope it wasn't Blanche. That would rather dampen my ardour. Would you believe it, my dear fellow, she wanted me to pay a visit to this countess and threaten her, but of course, I refused."

"Threaten her with what?"

"I didn't very clearly understand. It was something about some letters that Blanche had written, and which had fallen into the hands of the countess. Blanche wants to regain possession of them, and she seemed to think that I could assist her in obtaining them. However, I told her very plainly that the mission did not suit me, and then she insisted no further. On the contrary, we parted the best friends in the world."

"Well, believe me, I don't speak lightly; but I advise you to have nothing more to do with Blanche Pornic. She is a very attractive woman, but there are plenty of others equally charming; besides, there are circumstances that render any intimacy with her undesirable, and even dangerous just now. Dargental's tragical death has created a good deal of talk, and the authorities have begun an investigation. I know that Blanche has been questioned already, and maybe she may still be implicated in the affair."

"Hum! that would be serious; but excuse me, I see over there a worthy man whom I wish to introduce to you— Roch Plancoët, my poor father's foster brother."

"Madame Verdon just spoke of him to me."

"Then you already know that he is the best friend we have in the world. He has been devoted to my sister and myself from our earliest infancy. He might have made a fortune in the business—he was in a fair way of doing so—but he has come to live in Paris on an income of six thousand francs a year, because he couldn't exist without seeing Gabrielle. We will have a chat with him if you don't mind. Here, Plancoët!" The promenader looked up, recognised Albert, and hastened towards him. "How are you, old fellow?" asked the young lieutenant, slapping him familiarly on the shoulder. "You must take a glass of beer with us. Sit down. Do you see this gentleman? Well, he is Gabrielle's intended husband."

M. Plancoët did not seem to be very much surprised by this abrupt announcement, but he looked searchingly at George, who returned the scrutiny with interest. This faithful friend of the Verdon family seemed to be about fifty years of age, and he was still strong and hearty. His strong-features bespoke unusual energy, and strength of mind. His eyes were keen and intelligent, and his smile had much of the patient sweetness of a man accustomed to sacrifice himself for others. In short, his appearance was decidedly prepossessing, and George instantly conceived a strong liking to him. "I trust, sir," he said, almost affectionately, "that Mademoiselle Verdon's marriage will not part you from her. You will always be most welcome at my wife's house."

"I thank you for this assurance," replied M. Plancoët, quietly but earnestly, "though I must admit that I was not unprepared for it. Gabrielle has so often spoken of you, and always in such high terms, that I relied as implicitly upon your hospitality as you can rely upon my devotion."

"Monsieur Caumont doesn't doubt that, my dear Roch," interposed Albert. "I have told him all about you. But I have another piece of news for you—one that is much less agreeable in its nature."

"Your mother's intended marriage," said Plancoët, sadly. "That isn't necessary, my boy. She announced it to me this morning. But what about yourself, what have you been doing since I saw you last?—more than six months ago—for our meeting at the door of your mother's house does not count, as you merely said two or three words to me, and then rushed off like a madman."

"Tell you what I have been doing? Being bored to death—that is about all. If you think military life very enjoyable, you are greatly mistaken."

"You doubtless found it very dull while in garrison; but you seem to have been making up for it since your arrival in Paris. Your sister vainly expected you all the morning, and she is very cross with you in consequence."

"We are reconciled. Besides, although I dined at the Lion d'Or yesterday, I shall dine at home this evening."

"At the Lion d'Or!" repeated M. Plancoët, in astonishment. "You dined at the Lion d'Or yesterday?"

"Yes, old fellow. What is there so very astonishing about that? It's a good restaurant. My intended brother-in-law often patronizes it, I'm sure, though he probably goes alone, whereas I was in company with a very pretty woman."

"I don't patronize it often," answered George. "In fact, I have not been there since the day I lunched with my friend Puymirol."

"The gentleman whom Blanche pointed out to me yesterday!" exclaimed the lieutenant. "But she was at that lunch as well. She told me so."

"Yes, there were four of us. She was the only lady."

"And it was the very day of Monsieur Dargental's death. Blanche could talk of nothing else. You may have heard of that gentleman's murder, Plancoët?"

"No—that is to say, yes. It seems to me I did see something about it in the papers," stammered M. Plancoët, with the air of a man suddenly awakening from a dream. "Were you acquainted with him?"

"Not at all, but George, here, knew him well." The friend of the family now looked searchingly at George. "What the deuce is the matter with you to-day?" continued Albert. "You seem to be amazed at everything. Is there anything so very extraordinary in the fact that Caumont should have known that gentleman? His friend Puymirol was also acquainted with him, and so was the lady who dined with me yesterday."

"Speaking of my friend Puymirol," said George, turning to the lieutenant. "I am very uneasy about him, for he didn't return home last night. We live in the same house, you know, No. 14, Rue de Medicis?"

"Oh, he will turn up safely, no doubt. It isn't so strange for a young bachelor to stop out all night in Paris," added Albert, laughing. "By the way, you must bring him to see my mother. She will find a wife for him. But I forgot. She won't have time, as she intends to leave Paris immediately after your wedding."

"Puymirol will be my best man, probably."

"And Plancoët will certainly be one of my sister's witnesses, so that these gentlemen will have an opportunity of making each other's acquaintance. But the prospect does not seem to please you, Roch. You look dreadfully gloomy. Have you anything against the gentleman?"

"I!" exclaimed Plancoët. "Why! this is the first time I ever heard of him."

"Then why do you look so sulky? Ever since you have heard that he is likely to figure at the ceremony, your face has worn the same expression as it assumes when you see Rochas."

"You must be dreaming, my boy. The truth is, your proposal did not strike me very favourably, as I am much too old to serve as Gabrielle's witness. One of your comrades would be much more suitable. The old bring misfortune with them."

"Nonsense! On the contrary, you are a fetish. We have always prospered since we knew you."

"That isn't the opinion of every one," remarked M. Plancoët, pointedly.

George realised that Madame Verdon was the exception referred to, and he thought it time to conclude the interview. He had seen enough of M. Plancoët, and it seemed to him that the worthy man stared at him in a rather objectionable manner; besides, he was anxious to find out if Puymirol had returned home. "Excuse me for leaving you now," he said, pleasantly. "But I shall feel very uncomfortable until I see my friend again, and as I hate suspense, I am going to put an end to it by interviewing my doorkeeper."

"Of course," said Albert, "I also must go home if I want to avoid a scene. My mother is just in the humour to scold me, and Gabrielle may side with her, for she must be impatiently waiting to know what I think of you. She will probably subject me to a close examination; still you need have no fears as regards my replies. "But where are you going, Roch? Will you accompany me home?"

"It's impossible. I have some business to attend to—"

"As usual. The deuce take me, if I can imagine how you occupy your time. But it is no affair of mine. Good-bye, my dear brother-in-law, I hope to see you again soon."

The two young men exchanged a cordial pressure of the hand, while M. Plancoët contented himself with bowing to Gabrielle's future husband. The salute was very pleasant and deferential, but George somehow fancied that M. Plancoët seemed inclined to hold himself a little aloof, and that there was a slight cloud between them.

They separated, and George then hastened to the Rue de Medicis, where he learnt with no little consternation, that Puymirol had given no sign of life. Some serious accident must certainly have happened to him. In fact, it was a much more terrible matter than George supposed.

## V.

After his midnight mishap, Puymirol, still suffering from his fall, slowly and gloomily retraced his steps. What should he do with himself? He was in no humour to go to bed, and the thought occurred to him that he might perhaps still retrieve his losses at the gaming-table. The doors of his own club were closed against him until his outstanding debt was paid, but he knew other places easy of access, for in Paris there are plenty of private gambling-dens to which a man can gain admission by feeing the door-keeper, as Puymirol was well aware. Thus in his great need, the idea of again trying his luck occurred to him, and he did not lose a moment in carrying it into execution. But, alas, the thirty louis which still remained to him were speedily lost in an establishment of the Chaussée d'Antin; and Puymirol, disheartened and exhausted, left the card-room, and passing into an adjoining apartment flung himself upon a sofa. He felt that irresistible longing to sleep which so often follows upon great crises. His eyes closed in spite of all his efforts to keep them open, and in a few moments he fell into a profound slumber which no one at first disturbed, for at the gaming-table players don't trouble themselves about the wounded. He was still sleeping heavily when he was roughly shaken by a footman; and when he opened his eyes in bewilderment he found that it was broad daylight. "What time is it?" he inquired, with a yawn.

"Past eight o'clock," replied the footman sullenly. "All the other gentlemen left a long while ago; and I must set the room in order. This isn't a lodging house."

Puymirol felt strongly inclined to kick the fellow who had so rudely recalled him to the realities of life, but he restrained his wrath, and rose up without a word. He found his hat and overcoat in the cloak-room, and orthwith left the establishment, having decided to return home at once so as to see George and procure the letters, for his late reverses had discouraged him so much that he was now inclined to accept Madame de Lescombat's offer. He accordingly walked towards the boulevard. Paris was already astir; the passers-by jostled him on the side walk, and vehicles went rapidly to and fro. As he was hastening past a doorway he narrowly escaped stumbling over a boy who was lying there, more than half asleep. At this, he paused, with a muttered oath, and heard the urchin mumble a few words which he did not at first understand. Our friend was not in the best of humours by any means, and he felt highly incensed with the little fellow, whom he suspected of lying in wait to trip up unwary passers-by. "What did you say, you young rascal?" he cried savagely.

"Buy the official list," sleepily responded the lad, rubbing his eyes.

Seizing the little fellow by his coat collar, Puymirol set him on his feet in the twinkling of an eye. "Do you know," said he, "you very nearly broke my neck, and I have a great mind to call a policeman to take you to the station-house? What do you mean by going to sleep on the pavement?"

"It is not my fault, sir," sobbed the boy. "I dared not go home because I hadn't sold all the lists. Mother would have been sure to beat me. So I ran about the streets all the evening until I couldn't stand it any longer, and then I sat down here to rest, and fell asleep. Don't have me arrested, please don't. I am going to set to work again now, and perhaps I shall manage to sell what I've got left."

Puymirol was really kind-hearted, and the sight of the lad's distress so touched him, that he put his hand in his pocket. He found himself richer than he had supposed, for his pocket happened to contain a quantity of small silver, which had escaped the croupier's rake. "What have you got there?" he asked.

"Why, sir, I'm selling lists of the winning numbers of the Lottery of the Decorative Art Society. They cost only two sous apiece; buy one, sir."

"Well, here are five francs, my lad. You don't look to me as if you had much dinner yesterday. Go and get something to eat, and then go home to bed. You can take the money you have left to your mother, and she won't beat you."

The boy took the money, trying to falter out his thanks; and as Puymirol hastened on, he ran after him, and forced one of the lists of winning numbers into his hand, saying: "Please take it. It may bring you good luck, sir."

In Puymirol's present desperate plight the remark sounded very much like a sarcasm. Still he took the list, and as he went on his way he glanced at it mechanically, and beheld in large figures the number of the ticket which had won the grand prize of one hundred thousand francs.

"Number 115,815!" he murmured. "That is to say, there is now somewhere in Paris, or in the provinces, a fortunate mortal who paid a franc for a scrap of paper which he can now exchange for one hundred thousand francs in bank notes. And this lucky fellow is perhaps a millionaire who has more money than he knows what to do with already, whereas if I had one hundred thousand francs I should consider myself independent for life." So reflecting, Puymirol crumpled the list in his hand, and was about to throw it away, when a new idea flashed through his brain. "Why, I still have those tickets I found in the pocket-book. While I was chasing that rascal last night, I placed them in my waistcoat pocket. What if I should find one of the winning numbers among them? Let me see."

He drew out the little packet of tickets, some two dozen in number, and, stopping short behind a newspaper kiosk, he slowly unfolded them. As he glanced at the topmost ticket he could scarcely believe his eyes, for there was the number—the winning number printed in the centre of it. He read and re-read it, examined it again and again, and compared it, figure by figure, with the list in his other hand; but it was all quite true, he certainly had in his possession No. 115,815, which entitled its owner to the grand prize. He had nineteen francs in his pocket, nothing in his desk, and one hundred thousand francs between his fingers. The shock was so great and so unexpected, that, proof as he had always considered himself against emotion, he was obliged to lean against the newspaper kiosk for support. His brain reeled. But suddenly a fresh thought occurred to him. "Dash it! the ticket isn't mine! It belonged to Dargental. In fact, it is the only piece of property he left for his heirs, if he has any. I have no right to appropriate it. It would be a theft." Puymirol's face lengthened, but he quickly recovered himself. "A theft, no. I did not steal it; I found it, or rather it was thrown to me, which amounted to the same thing as giving it to me."

This sophistry did not deceive him, however. He had invented it to quiet his conscience; but he realised how shallow it was. Then he thought of consulting Caumont, but he felt a presentiment that George would advise him to give up the ticket; and he did not care for advice which he did not intend to follow. But where and how was this grand prize payable? Would it only be necessary to show this triumphant No. 115,815 at the lottery office to convert it into bank notes? One of these questions was answered on the back of the ticket. He there read that the office of the Lottery of the Society of Decorative Arts was at the Palais de l'Industrie, in the Champs Elysées, Door No. 4. Puymirol's position was too desperate for him to indulge in much reflection. He made a nervous gesture as if to say: "I must cross the Rubicon," and then he replaced the tickets in his pocket. However, before going to the lottery office, he must set his toilet right. Still, this was easily managed. There were some Turkish baths hard by, and after indulging in the wholesome luxury of Oriental ablutions, he proceeded in due course to a fashionable barber's, where he was shaved, cosmetiqued, and perfumed, so that he would have been presentable anywhere, although he had not changed his linen. These preparations occupied him until eleven o'clock, and then, after partaking of a light breakfast, which exhausted his remaining funds, he hastened to the Palais de l'Industrie. At door No. 4, which seemed to him very like the gate of Paradise, he found a liveried footman talking with two men whom he took for favourites of fortune, who, like himself, had come to receive their money. He explained why he wished to speak to the secretary, and the attendant having gazed at him with admiring envy, told him to walk upstairs. The two persons who had been waiting, followed in his wake, and they all three entered a large ante-room on the first floor. A clerk rose on seeing them, and Puymirol was about to repeat his statement when one of the other fellows hastily approached the clerk, took him aside, and said a few words to him in a low tone; thereupon the clerk immediately opened a side door, and the man passed out and disappeared.

Turning to Puymirol, the clerk then inquired what he wanted, and on learning that he had come to cash a winning ticket, he at once opened a door leading into the office proper, where Puymirol found two prepossessing-looking gentlemen. One of them sat in an arm-chair, while the other occupied a stool at the end of the same table, and had a large leather case, such as is employed for the conveyance of documents, before him. "To whom have I the honour of speaking?" inquired the gentleman in the arm-chair.

"I am the holder of ticket No. 115,815, which is mentioned as having won one hundred thousand francs at your last drawing."

"I congratulate you, sir. Will you take a seat?"

Puymirol accepted the invitation; but in spite of his gracious reception, he felt ill at ease in the presence of these two persons. When a man has not a clear conscience, he sees danger everywhere, and Puymirol almost fancied himself a culprit arraigned before an investigating magistrate and his secretary. It was necessary to exhibit the ticket, however, so he drew the whole packet from his pocket and handed it to the gentleman in the arm-chair, who unfolded it, and examined the tickets one after another. "Here are some that do not interest us," he remarked: "the Tunisian Lottery, the Amsterdam Lottery."

"Yes," replied Puymirol, "I take a chance or two in all of them, but so far I have never won anything."

The official continued his examination, and finally lighted upon No. 115,815. This he examined closely, first upon one side, and then upon the other, and finally passed it to the gentleman seated at the end of the table. "Excuse this close examination," he remarked to Puymirol. "It not infrequently happens that spurious tickets are presented to us; that is to say, tickets of which the numbers have been altered."

"That is not the case with mine, I suppose?"

"No, sir. It is a little soiled, but it has not been tampered with."

"Then I can draw the amount?"

"There are certain formalities which must be gone through first of all. Will you give me your name and address?"

Puymirol coloured slightly. "Is this indispensable?" he asked. "I don't care to have my name in the papers. If it became known that I had won this prize," he added, a little nervously, "I should be beset on every side by requests for money. All my impecunious friends would make demands upon my purse, and my hundred thousand francs wouldn't last long."

"Oh! you need have no fears, sir. We shall not publish your name. This isn't the first time that winners have requested us not to give their names, and we have always complied with such requests, although, by doing so, we miss an excellent advertisement for our lottery. You need not, therefore, object to giving us your name and address. They will be recorded upon our books, but no one will be allowed to see them."

"That is all I ask. My name is Adhémar de Puymirol. I am a medical student, and I reside at No. 14 Rue de Medicis."

"Very well, sir, we will make a note of it. I forgot to mention that you would be obliged to give this information, in any case, for no winner can draw a penny of his money without giving a receipt to which his address must be appended."

"I fancied that it would only be necessary to present the ticket at your office so as to obtain the money, but I am ready and willing to give a receipt for it."

The gentleman took no notice of this hint. He seemed to have become suddenly absorbed in the examination of some papers; however, the person whom Adhémar had taken for a secretary, looked up, and, with his eyes fixed searchingly on the applicant's face, he curtly asked: "How old are you?"

"What difference can my age possibly make? I have attained my majority, as you see, and that is all that is necessary to make my receipt perfectly valid."

"Where were you born?"

"What business is that of yours?" replied Adhémar, exasperated by these strange questions.

"You refuse to answer, then?"

"Yes, certainly. I came here to draw the money due to me. I don't intend to be cross examined like some criminal."

"Be careful, I am a commissary of police."

Puymirol turned pale. He realised, at last, that he had plunged blindly into a frightful abyss, and that his imprudence was about to cost him dear. He was resolved to defend himself to the last, however. "I was not aware that the managers of this popular lottery required the assistance of police officials in the performance of their duties," he retorted. "This precaution will hardly favour the sale of tickets, should it become known to the public, and I will take good care to inform people about it."

"You are speaking to a magistrate, remember. Tell me where, and when, you purchased this ticket?'

"At a tobacconist's, probably."

"What tobacconist's?"

"The deuce take me if I can remember. I purchased between twenty and thirty tickets, and in a dozen different places. They are all here on the table."

"Yes, I see you have brought them all. It is strange that the idea of detaching the winning ticket did not occur to you. One can not think of everything, however."

"I brought the package exactly as I took it from my pocket-book."

"Have you that pocket-book about you?"

"No," stammered Puymirol, disconcerted by this question, which he might have foreseen, however. "I left it at home."

"Of course, great as your audacity may be, you would hardly dare to produce that. It bears other initials than yours."

"Produce it if you can," retorted Puymirol, imprudently.

"I understand. You have no fear of its being produced; you have destroyed it."

This time the commissary had made a mistake, and a suspicion that had flashed across Puymirol's mind a few moments before, was effectually dispelled. He had fancied that his assailant of the previous night might have been set upon his track by the police, who had taken forcible possession of the pocket-book, by orders of his superiors. "I do not understand you, unfortunately," said Adhémar. "But let us put an end to this. What are you aiming at?"

"Well, a crime was committed in Paris about a fortnight ago. A well-known gentleman, a man of fashion, was murdered at midday, in his rooms. You must have heard of the affair?"

"Yes, through the papers."

"Well, the gentleman's valet was arrested; but, as there was no evidence against him, he has been released. The murderer has not only escaped detection so far, but the motive that prompted the crime has not yet been discovered. All that has been ascertained is that the victim always carried a pocket-book, of which a full description has been given, and that this pocket-book has disappeared."

"All this is very interesting," sneered Puymirol. "The pocket-book probably contained a large sum of money?"

"That is the general supposition, but one can not be sure. One thing, however, is certain; it contained several tickets of this lottery, and among this gentleman's private papers, a list of these tickets was found. It occurred to the investigating magistrate that he might utilise this information in the improbable event of one of these particular tickets winning a prize, and being presented for payment by the murderer. It was one chance in a million, and yet it has occurred. As soon as the investigating magistrate ascertained that one of these tickets had won the grand prize, he gave me orders to come here with two detectives. Now, you must understand the situation. What have you to say?"

"Nothing."

"Your silence is equivalent to a confession of guilt. You admit, then, that you purloined these tickets after killing the man who had them about his person?"

"I admit nothing of the kind."

"Oh! it is patent that you took them from the body of your victim; and you had the courage to open the pocket-book immediately after murdering that unfortunate man. Look at this ticket. The mark of your bloody fingers is still upon it."

As the commissary spoke he spread the ticket out upon the table and pointed to a couple of pale red stains upon the back of it and which Puymirol had not perceived when he had looked at the ticket on the boulevard. However he made no attempt to refute the commissary's arguments. He had decided to defend himself in a different way. "So you really accuse me of murder and robbery?" he asked.

"I have merely stated the facts and the conclusions one must naturally draw from them. It is for you to prove that my deductions are false. Now, do you still persist in declaring that you purchased the tickets in a cigar shop?"

"No," was Adhémar's reluctant response. "I found them in a cab a fortnight ago."

"And you kept them until now?"

"I attached very little importance to the occurrence. Lottery tickets are seldom of any value."

"Before the drawing, perhaps so; but afterwards when one of them has won a prize, it is very different."

"I admit that I yielded to the temptation of trying to profit by what seemed almost a godsend; I had no idea of doing so until this morning, however, when a list of the winning numbers happened to fall into my hands. I had the tickets in my pocket at the time, and impelled by a very natural curiosity to compare them with the list, I saw that the first prize had been won by No. 115,815. I yielded to the temptation which I regret, and I am certainly sufficiently punished."

"Why did you not inform Monsieur Robergeot of the finding of these tickets?" inquired the commissary, after a prolonged pause.

"Who is Monsieur Robergeot?"

"The investigating magistrate who sent for you on the day after the murder. I have his report here. You see I know everything."

"But I had no reason to suppose that this ticket had ever belonged to Dargental. The magistrate said nothing that would lead me to think so. He only asked me what I saw on entering the room in which the body was lying, and what I thought of the valet's connection with the affair."

"At that time the memorandum had not been found. But from

what you say, the tickets were in your possession when you were first examined."

Puymirol bit his lip, but it was too late to retract this imprudent admission. "Yes," he replied at last. "They had been in my possession since the previous day, though at the time I forgot all about them."

"You picked them up in a cab you said. In that case, it is natural to suppose that the murderer dropped them there, or that he left them there intentionally. He certainly did not murder Monsieur Dargental to obtain possession of them. However, where did you take this cab?"

"At the cab-stand near my house outside the Luxembourg."

"And it took you where?"

"To the Lion d'Or restaurant where Dargental had asked me to meet him. He was giving a lunch that day to several friends."

"At what hour did you reach the restaurant?"

"About noon."

"And the crime must have been committed at about eleven o'clock. It is strange that the murderer should have driven back to the Odéon almost to your very door."

Puymirol made no reply. He felt that he was not capable of contending with the commissary. "Did you take the number of this cab?" added the official.

"No. I had no special reason for taking it."

"Excuse me: had you done so, you might have questioned the driver, and have ascertained where he had left the passenger who had dropped the lottery tickets. It is true that you were not anxious to find him, as you had already decided to keep them." Puymirol flushed, and hung his head. To clear himself of the charge of murder he had placed himself in such a position that he could not deny a fraudulent intention. "It is a great pity," continued the commissary. "The driver's testimony would be of great importance, for the magistrate is not obliged to take your word, and if you can produce no witness— Were you alone in the cab?"

This time Puymirol hesitated. It was too great a risk to mention George Caumont's name, for George, who was ignorant of the real situation of affairs, would simply tell the truth, and then the pocket-book, which Puymirol no longer possessed, would come into question; and besides, George would probably hand over the letters. Perhaps he would even tell the magistrate that one of the letters was written by the Countess de Lescombat, and one of the others probably by Blanche Pornic, in which case the least that could happen to Puymirol would be a conviction for perjury; so hoping to avert this new danger by a falsehood, he replied unblushingly: "I was alone."

"There is nothing left for us, then, but to try and find the driver," replied the commissary coldly, "and we may, perhaps, succeed in finding him. We have the exact date, as well as the point of departure, and the place of destination. We will make inquiries at the office of the cab company, and at all the livery stables. If the driver remembers the occurrence he can give us the clue we want."

Puymirol knew perfectly well that the driver would recollect the occurrence, as he had given the mysterious stranger who had purloined the pocket-book full information about it, so seeing that he was getting deeper and deeper into the mire, he decided to make a bold attempt to cut the interview short. "I reproach myself bitterly for having yielded to a temptation for which I blush," he said. "You must blame me very severely, but I hope you will not carry matters to extremes. I belong to a respectable family, and my past life is without a stain. I shall be at your disposal, of course, but I ask your permission to withdraw."

"My powers are more limited than you suppose," said the commissary gravely. "The magistrate will pay due attention to your explanation, but you must give it to him in person. He must now be at the Palais de Justice, and I will accompany you there."

"Nothing would please me better. I thought of calling at his office to-day, and as you are kind enough to accompany me—"

"It is my duty."

The commissary then rang. One of the detectives who had remained in the ante-room entered, and received orders to fetch a cab: then, taking up his case of documents, the commissary left the room in company with Puymirol, whose wonted assurance had nearly deserted him. They found the cab at the door, and entered it, one of the detectives climbing upon the box, and seating himself beside the driver. The journey was a silent one, and ended upon the Quai de l'Horloge, at the entrance to the court-yard of the Conciergerie. "Where are you taking me?" asked Puymirol. "Monsieur Robergeot's office is in the building facing the boulevard."

"You will soon be summoned there," replied the commissary. "But I must see him before you do, and in the meanwhile I must consign you to the dépôt of the Prefecture of Police."

## VI.

On the day following Puymirol's arrest—for Puymirol was really and truly arrested—George Caumont, who had passed a very restless and uncomfortable night, was awakened at an early hour by his prospective brother-in-law. "I have come to propose a morning ride, my dear fellow," said Albert. "It is generally a thankless task to arouse a friend from sleep, but when you hear my reasons I am sure that you will forgive me. You know my mare, Verdurette, that enabled me to win a prize at the show. Well, I have come here on her back and a friend of mine has lent me two other mounts,—a very gentle animal suited to a lady, and a hack which would do very well for you. But I must tell you that last night at dinner, my sister obtained my mother's permission to take a ride in the Bois de Boulogne this morning, escorted by her betrothed and by your humble servant. Fortunately Rochas wasn't there to interfere, and it was decided that all three of us should start at half-past nine this morning. So make haste, the three horses are already standing, saddled and bridled, in our court-yard, and Gabrielle is awaiting you on the balcony. However, if the proposal doesn't please you—"

"On the contrary, I should be delighted, only I intended to spend my morning in trying to ascertain what had become of my friend Puymirol."

"What! hasn't he made his appearance yet?" exclaimed Albert, gaily. "To spend two nights out is dissipation, indeed; but I see nothing alarming it. Besides, you can do nothing. Come with us to the Bois. We can spend a couple of hours there very pleasantly, and when you return you will probably find your friend here waiting for you."

George was not convinced, but he could not tell Albert that Puymirol had become involved in dangerous schemes which might have terminated in a catastrophe. "All right," said he, "I should never forgive myself if I disappointed Mademoiselle Verdon. I will dress at once. If you like to smoke a cigar, there are some good ones in that box on the mantel-shelf." And, thereupon, George hastily dressed, and was soon ready to depart.

The house where Madame Verdon resided was only a few steps from the Rue de Medicis, and on turning the corner of the Boulevard Saint-Michel the two friends perceived the mother and daughter on the balcony. The mother was arrayed in a showy morning dress, the daughter in a dark green habit. The three horses were waiting in the court-yard, and George recognised at a glance the animal intended for him, a tall chestnut, with a spirit of mischief in his eyes. Gabrielle hastened down, and soon stood beside the young men. Her eyes were shining, her cheeks rosy, and her lips smiling. She extended her gloved hand to her betrothed, who pressed a respectful kiss upon it, as she gaily said: "So here you are at last. I was becoming so impatient. I began to fear that we should be obliged to abandon our expedition, and I really believe I should have cried with disappointment and vexation."

"I am truly sorry to have kept you waiting, mademoiselle, and—"

"Come, come; there's no time to lose. Let me mount you, Gabrielle," said Albert, and in the twinkling of an eye his sister was in the saddle.

The gentlemen then duly mounted in turn, and having saluted Madame Verdon they rode out of the yard. To reach the Boulevard St. Germain, the best road to the Bois, they had to cross the Rue de Medicis, where George resided, and scarcely were they in sight of that thoroughfare than the lieutenant turned to Caumont, exclaiming: "Why, what a crowd there is about your door! Can the house be on fire?"

It was not a fire, but something unusual was certainly going on. There were now two cabs in front of the house, and a policeman was waving back an eager crowd of people. A presentiment that all this commotion was in some way connected with Puymirol flashed across George's mind. Had his friend been brought home, wounded, dead, perhaps? "Try to find out what the matter is!" urged Albert, whereupon George checked his horse and spoke to a man who was moving away, exasperated by not having seen anything.

"Oh! the fools make such a fuss about nothing!" replied the fellow, shrugging his shoulders. "The police are searching somebody's rooms, that is all."

George was struck dumb with astonishment. What could this mean? Whose apartments were they searching? And as he asked himself this question it suddenly occurred to him that this search might be for the famous letters. The magistrate might have learned that they had fallen into Puymirol's hands, and have decided to institute a search for them. This thought worried George, for these letters were in his rooms, and if he entered the house to make any further inquiries he would certainly be putting his head into the lion's mouth, for the doorkeeper would hardly fail to inform the police of his arrival. In that case, what should he say and do to assist his friend? George did not understand Puymirol's situation, but he realised that an imprudent answer might ruin him. By keeping out of sight he would at least incur no danger of contradicting Puymirol's statements. He, Caumont, was as yet in no way connected with the affair, and in his absence no one would venture to break into his rooms to search for the letters, whereas, if he showed himself, he might be plied with questions to which he could only give unsatisfactory replies, and he might even finally be obliged to let the officials search his apartments. Worst of all, if he should be detained, Gabrielle would learn that her betrothed was mixed up in a most unfortunate affair, and the excursion to the Bois would have to be relinquished, and perhaps the marriage as well. So it was best not to interfere, at least, for the present.

The brother and sister had remained in the middle of the street, watching the crowd with evident curiosity. "Well!" inquired the lieutenant, as soon as George resumed his place on Gabrielle's left, "what is going on?"

"Nothing that can interest you in the least. The police have made a raid upon the apartments of some one in the house, it seems."

"Indeed! Upon whose?"

"I do not know. The only person that I am acquainted with in the house is Puymirol."

"And it can not be his apartments they are searching."

"Nor mine, as I am not there," responded George.

"Where are your windows?" asked Gabrielle.

"On the third floor, mademoiselle."

"But, then, the police *are* in your place, for, look, there is a commissary with his sash at that open window."

"Oh! my rooms are to the right—on the same floor, it's true," said George, who, to his horror, had recognised the window, where the commissary stood, as that of Puymirol's bedroom.

"Well, let us proceed, then," said Albert. "If we loiter in this way, we shall never reach our destination, and I am anxious to see the Bois at its best."

This proposal was eminently satisfactory to George, who was anxious to get away from the spot as soon as possible. But all his enjoyment was spoiled. His cheerfulness had vanished; however, Gabrielle failed to notice the change, at least, for the time being, as at this moment Albert asked her: "Have you seen Roch since yesterday?"

"No, and I am very much afraid that I shall not see much of him until after my marriage. Monsieur Rochas called this morning expressly to beg mamma not to receive our old friend any longer."

"What business is it of his, pray? and what has he to say against Plancoët, whose little finger is worth more than Rochas's whole body?"

"He pretends that our old friend is a dangerous character. To hear him, one would suppose that poor Roch had committed any number of crimes—Roch who would not harm a mouse, and who has sacrificed himself for others ever since he came into the world."

"Well, no matter," rejoined Albert, "we shall soon be rid of Rochas and have Plancoët all to ourselves. Now, my children, we are upon the macadamized pavement, and we have plenty of room into the bargain, so suppose we trot a little."

They trotted on along the boulevard and up the Champs Elysées without their progress being impeded. But in the Bois there were scores of riders of either sex and also a number of carriages. Albert began disdainfully criticising the horsemanship of those around him, and Gabrielle laughed heartily at his comments, and began to feel surprised that George remained so serious. Such was the throng that all along the Allée des Poteaux they were obliged to walk their horses, which was hardly to Albert's liking. "Come," said he, at last, "I've had enough of this. I don't care to stare for ever at all these fine ladies and swells. Suppose we make for the Allée de Longchamps, and have a canter there. Verdurette is becoming restive."

The suggestion was adopted. They turned their horses' heads in the direction of the lake, but they had hardly proceeded a hundred yards when George saw his friend Charles Balmer approaching on a handsome thoroughbred. Balmer expressed his delight at the meeting by an expressive gesture, and, reining in his horse, he abruptly said to George: "My dear fellow, I must have a talk with you. It's serious. Apologize to your friends, and join me at the chalet at the end of the lake. I will wait for you there." And thereupon he rode off.

"That gentleman is not very polite," exclaimed the lieutenant. "He certainly might have touched his hat to Gabrielle. What did he say to you?"

Gabrielle, who had heard Balmer distinctly, looked at George inquisitively. She did not like to question him, but she awaited his answer with no little anxiety. George, who was greatly embarrassed, reluctantly replied:

"He asked me to join him at the end of the lake; and I would much rather remain with you."

"Is he a friend of yours?" inquired Gabrielle.

"No, merely a club acquaintance."

"But if what he wants to say to you is important, you might leave us, and join us by-and-by at the Porte Maillot," insisted Gabrielle. "Have you any idea what he wants to speak to you about?"

"I have an idea, mademoiselle. He probably wants to give me some information in reference to Puymirol."

"The friend whose absence has caused you so much uneasiness?"

"Yes, mademoiselle. This gentleman is well acquainted with him; and I fancy he knows what has become of him."

"You must go, then."

"Leave you! Oh, no."

"But you need not leave us for long, and who knows but what M. de Puymirol may need you. I should never forgive myself for detaining you if he required your assistance; and this gentleman has perhaps come for you at his request. Go at once, pray."

George was greatly perplexed. The idea of leaving his betrothed so unceremoniously was most distasteful to him; but on the other hand, he suspected that Balmer had something pressing to communicate. Puymirol's safety was, perhaps, at stake, for since George had witnessed the raid upon the house in the Rue de Medicis, he felt almost certain that his friend had been arrested; now, Balmer, as he well knew, was on excellent terms with the investigating magistrate, and might speak a good word for Puymirol if he needed one. "You need not hesitate if the matter is of the slightest importance, my dear fellow," now exclaimed Albert, seeing his prospective brother-in-law's embarrassment. "I can see Gabrielle safely home, without your assistance, and as your conversation with this gentleman may be a lengthy one, we won't wait for you at the Porte Maillot. Vulcan, your steed, is quartered at Tattersall's, so just leave him there in charge of one of the ostlers on your way home."

"And come and see us as soon as you can," added Gabrielle. "I am anxious to hear about your friend." Then to make George feel perfectly at ease, she touched her horse lightly with the whip and cantered away, closely followed by her brother.

George decided not to follow them, but turned his horse's head in the direction which Balmer had taken. In a few moments he had reached the Chalet Café, in front of which sat Balmer, regaling himself with a glass of absinthe, and smoking a huge cigar. Springing to the ground, George intrusted his horse to an urchin, and seated himself beside Balmer, of whom, without the least ceremony, he inquired, "Why do you want to see me?"

"Why?" was the reply. "You must surely have guessed that I want to talk to you about Puymirol. When did you see him last?"

"On the day before yesterday, at the Palais de l'Industrie."

"Have you any idea where he went afterwards?"

"I think he went to Madame de Lescombat's; but he hasn't returned home since, and I feel very anxious about him."

"He has had good reasons for not returning. You will recollect that on the day before yesterday, I told you that my friend Robergeot was in possession of a document which might assist him in discovering Dargental's murderer."

"It seems to me that you did tell me something of the kind," said Caumont.

"Well, the document in question was in reality a small memorandum-book. Dargental, as you know, was an inveterate gambler, but he was also a very methodical man, and so whenever he won or lost any money or made a purchase—such as a lottery ticket, he made a note of the number in this book. He carried several lottery tickets about with him in the pocket-book which the murderer stole from him, and this was recorded in his memorandum-book. So Robergeot said to himself: 'If by any extraordinary chance one of the tickets enumerated in this list should win a prize, the murderer will perhaps be foolish enough to claim the money.' Well, this is exactly what has happened. Ticket No. 115,815, which headed Dargental's list, won a prize of a hundred thousand francs at the last drawing of the lottery of the Decorative Art Society; so Robergeot immediately despatched a commissary of police and two detectives to the lottery office with orders to arrest the holder of the ticket, if he ventured to present himself. He did present himself yesterday morning—and in the person of our friend Adhémar de Puymirol."

"Puymirol!" exclaimed George, "it's impossible!"

"This much, at least, is certain: Puymirol has been in prison for nearly two days now."

"And you haven't told your friend, the magistrate, that Puymirol could not possibly be Dargental's murderer? You know we were breakfasting with him at the very time when the crime was committed."

"Robergeot knows that, but the fact that the missing tickets were in Puymirol's possession can not be disputed. This attempt at fraud on his part surprises you, I see, as much as it does me," continued Balmer; "but I account for it by the fact that Puymirol was most desperately hard up. He owed ten thousand francs at the club, to my certain knowledge, and hadn't a penny to meet his obligations with. He must have lost his senses in consequence, besides, he couldn't know that the authorities had a list of Dargental's tickets, and that the police were lying in wait for him at the lottery office. As regards that matter I can almost excuse him, for, after all, he injured no one as Dargental was dead; and a man whose past life has always been blameless may be forgiven for a momentary weakness. Indeed, if this were the only charge against him, the matter could be hushed up, but there is the murder—"

"But no one can really believe him guilty of that. An incontestable *alibi* can be established."

"Yes; but it is also necessary to prove that Puymirol had no knowledge of the murder. Now, everything seems to indicate that he was aware of it. If not, how did he come into possession of that pocket-book containing the tickets?"

An answer rose to George's lips. He merely had to relate the adventure on the Place du Carrousel to explain the mystery, but the fear of contradicting some of Puymirol's statements deterred him; besides, he did not care to tell the story to an erratic person like Balmer. He must relate it to the investigating magistrate if there were no other means of saving Puymirol. However, realizing that he, first of all, needed further information, he asked: "How does Puymirol explain the fact that these tickets were in his possession?"

"He pretends that he found them in a cab."

"Then he denies having seen anything of the pocket-book?"

"Absolutely; he was searched and it wasn't found on his person; but the strangest thing about it all is that he says he found the tickets on the very day of Dargental's death, and in the cab that took him to the Lion d'Or, He did not notice the number of the vehicle, and he declares he was alone; but it seems to me that you both arrived at the restaurant at the same time."

"It doesn't follow that I drove there with him," replied George, evasively.

"You can tell that to Robergeot, for he will certainly question you. I am surprised that he has not sent for you before now. They are looking for the cab-driver, and will surely find him sooner or later. As for the pocket-book, Robergeot thought that Puymirol might have left it at home, so he ordered his rooms to be searched this morning. I am surprised that you are ignorant of that point, as you both reside in the same house."

"I left home very early. But did the officers find anything suspicious?"

"I don't know yet, but I shall soon; that is, if my friend Robergeot does not begin to distrust me now that things are looking so badly for Puymirol. He knows that we are both well acquainted with him, you especially, and between ourselves, I should not be surprised if your rooms were searched as well, for Robergeot may suspect Puymirol of having concealed the pocket-book there."

"Not with my knowledge and consent," said George.

"Oh! even if Puymirol were guilty, he wouldn't have made you his confidant, of course, Still, if I were in your place, I would find out what occurred in the Rue de Medicis at once, that is, unless you will come and lunch with me."

"No, thank you," replied George. "I shall take your advice, and return home without delay; but I rely upon your assistance in getting Puymirol out of this scrape."

"I will do what I can, but it won't be much I'm afraid; you, on the contrary, may perhaps be able to give evidence which will lead to his speedy release."

"You can at least ask your friend, Monsieur Robergeot, to grant me permission to see Puymirol at the dépôt."

"I will do so, of course; but I doubt if he will consent. But there is nothing to prevent you from calling on him in person if you like. He is at his office every afternoon."

"Is the affair known at the club?"

"Not in all its details, but a rumour of Puymirol's arrest has got about, and as his debts remain unpaid, you have no time to lose if you care to prevent a scandal. If you want to see me again I shall be at the club, between four and seven."

Springing upon his horse, George then galloped off, leaving Balmer to finish his absinthe. Ten minutes later, he left his steed at Tattersall's, and jumping into a cab, ordered the jehu to drive him with all speed to the Rue de Medicis. He took the precaution to alight at some distance from his door, however, so as not to attract the attention of the police, if they should still be about, but he soon had the satisfaction of finding that the crowd had dispersed, and that the vehicles which had brought the officers were no longer there. On entering the house, he went straight to the door-keeper, who on seeing him, exclaimed: "Ah, sir, what an unfortunate affair! You had no sooner gone out this morning than a magistrate, accompanied by a number of policemen, came here with Monsieur de Puymirol, who was under arrest."

"Puymirol! arrested!" cried George, feigning surprise. "This is incredible! What charge can there be against him?"

"I don't know, sir," replied the porter. "I tried to talk with the policemen who stood on guard in the street, but they wouldn't give me any information."

"But why did they bring Puymirol here?"

"So that he might be present when his apartments were searched, I suppose. They entered his rooms with him, and they rummaged about everywhere, even in the mattresses. I don't know what they were looking for, but I do know that they found nothing, and that they seemed terribly disappointed."

"How did Puymirol look while they searched his place?"

"He looked as if he were saying: 'Amuse yourself; break open the locks, and empty the drawers. You will only have your labour for your pains.' He scarcely deigned to give them an answer when they spoke to him."

"He must be the victim of some mistake. He is quite incapable of any crime."

"That is exactly what I said to the commissary of police, when he asked me for information about your friend."

"Did he say anything about me?" inquired George, eagerly.

"No; your name was not mentioned. He did not even seem to be aware of your existence. If I might venture to give you a little advice, sir, you had better not mix yourself up in this affair. Your friend will get out of the scrape without any assistance; and I have an idea that he prefers to do so; for if he had wanted your help, he would have inquired where you were, or have asked to see you."

This was not a bad argument; at least, it furnished George with abundant food for reflection. On reaching his rooms, he found them exactly as he had left them. He hastened to the desk in which he had locked up the letters. They were still there, and in his perplexity his first idea was to annihilate them. Indeed, he actually lighted a candle with that object. On reflection, however, it occurred to him that although the discovery of these letters, if his—Caumont's—rooms were searched, might aggravate Puymirol's situation, they might also be the means of saving him, by forcing him to tell the truth, instead of maintaining a dangerous silence out of consideration for the Countess de Lescombat, whose reputation was hardly worth defending. Would it not be better to take them to the magistrate? But in that case, both Madame de Lescombat and Blanche Pornic would be mixed up in the affair; and although George cared but little as to what befell the countess, he could not forget that Albert, his prospective brother-in-law, was the actress's admirer, and that he would certainly take her defence. The young officer was indeed so impetuous that he might fight the police agents sent to arrest her, and get himself lodged in jail! And what a blow that would be for Gabrielle. At last in his perplexity, George thought of a plan which seemed tolerably feasible. He resolved to go and see Blanche Pornic. As Albert was to lunch with his mother and sister, there was no fear of meeting him in the Avenue de Messine. "I shall question her, and question her closely," said Caumont to himself. "It will depend entirely upon her answers whether I return her letter to her, or hand it over to the investigating magistrate. At all events I must see that official to-day. The straight road is always the shortest and safest." Thereupon putting the letters in his pocket, George started off upon his campaign.

## VII.

Blanche Pornic occupied a handsome suite of rooms on the first floor of a stylish house in the Avenue de Messine, and when George arrived there he found her reclining upon a divan, studying a part in a new play in which she was shortly to perform. "So you have come to see me at last!" she exclaimed. "You have done wisely, for I had about made up my mind to pay you a visit, even at the risk of meeting your friend Puymirol, who can't bear the sight of me. Take a seat here, near me," she continued, "I have a host of things to tell you. I know now that the charming young girl, who engrossed your attention the other day at the horse-show, is Albert's sister, and I suppose she has introduced you to her brother."

"Never mind all that," said George, somewhat harshly. "I have come to talk with you about Dargental's death. Do you know who is accused of the murder?"

"His valet, I heard. But that's absurd unless, indeed, the fellow were in the pay of that Madame de Lescombat."

"What! you think it was she who—"

"I haven't the slightest doubt of it. I told you so the other day, you recollect?"

"Upon what is this opinion based?"

"Upon something I have seen, a letter of hers which Dargental himself showed me one day after a quarrel he had with this woman. I'm sure too that he kept it."

"What were its contents?"

"Oh! it alluded to a secret which she had confided to him. She had poisoned her husband, I fancy, and feared that Dargental would denounce her. It was only from fear that she consented to marry him, for though she was crazy about him at first, she finally hated him. And so to escape becoming his wife, she had him murdered, I'm sure of it."

"By whom, pray?"

"By some scoundrel who was no doubt instructed to secure the letter, as Dargental's pocket-book is missing."

"Haven't you yourself ever written to Dargental?"

"Oh! yes I have. A hundred times, as I have already told you. I even confessed to you that he had in his possession a letter which I had often begged him to return to me, and which he had promised to give me during the lunch at the Lion d'Or."

"And did this note contain anything of a compromising nature?"

"Decidedly. For I acknowledged in it that I had committed—well, a crime to do him a service."

"And if this avowal should fall into the hands of an investigating magistrate, what then?"

"He would naturally suppose that I instigated Dargental's murder. It might cause me a great deal of trouble, still I think I should succeed in proving my innocence. As for the matter to which I was stupid enough to allude in the letter, would you like to know what it was?" George had not expected to hear Blanche talk in this strain, but he was all ears. "I am not trying to make myself out any better than I really am," she continued, "and I frankly admit that I am capable of almost anything when I am in love with any one; but what I did was simply this. One day Dargental, whom I was then dreadfully in love with, came to me in a state of mind bordering on frenzy. He had just lost forty thousand francs, and he had not a penny left to meet his obligations. This meant expulsion from his club, and utter ruin, for he lived by play. At any other time, I would have given him a cheque upon my banker, as I had often done before, but this happened just after the crash of two years ago, when I feared that I myself was ruined, and a rascally picture dealer had just attached some twenty thousand francs I had in the bank. However, Dargental absolutely needed the money, and I did not know which way to turn. To be sure, I might have asked old Prince Sourine for it—he was an ardent admirer of mine, and worth his millions—but he was furiously angry with me because I had preferred Pierre to him. His signature was good for any amount, and I had numerous specimens of it in my desk, for he was in the habit of writing me the most grandiloquent epistles. Well, Dargental finally proposed that I should forge the prince's signature upon a note which he was sure of being able to discount with this indorsement."

"And you consented?" asked George in amazement.

"I would have done even worse, had he asked me. As it was, I forged the name of Alexis Ivanovitch, Prince Sourine, on the back of the note. Dargental obtained fifty thousand francs by it, and the money brought him good luck. He won immense sums at baccarat shortly afterwards, and was able to take up the note before it became due. But he did not return it to me. He probably wished to retain it as a weapon against me, in case I ever quarrelled with him. However, I finally discovered that he was playing me false with that Madame de Lescombat, so one morning I paid him a visit, and compelled him to burn the note in my presence. But I was fool enough at the time not to ask for the letter in which I had alluded to this affair. When I did remember it, I urged him to return it to me. Did he really intend to give it to me at the Lion d'Or as he promised? I doubt it. At all events, death prevented him from doing so, and I suppose it is locked up somewhere with that note he showed me from Madame de Lescombat, and it would not surprise me to hear that both of them had been found."

"And what if Albert should hear this story?" asked George.

"You surely do not think of telling him!" cried Blanche. "That *would* be mean. But now I understand. You have my letter, and you have come to sell it to me. How much do you want for it?"

George started up, pale with anger. "Do you take me for Dargental?" he asked, sternly. "You have associated so much with scoundrels of his stamp, that you think all men are like him. I will convince you to the contrary, and you shall bitterly repent having insulted me in this manner."

"Forgive me," replied Blanche. "I care so much for Albert that the fear of losing him upsets me completely. You mustn't tell him about my former infatuation for this unscrupulous man, and that I committed a forgery to save him. I confessed my crime, if crime it be, to you, because I trusted in your honour."

"I did not ask you to do so," said George, quickly.

"That is true. I was imprudent enough to accuse myself, still, I am sure that you won't betray my confidence. If you have my letter, take it to the investigating magistrate, if you like, but not one word to Albert, pray."

"It will be my duty to enlighten him."

"Because you expect to be his brother-in-law? Oh, don't deny it. Mademoiselle Verdon would not have walked about with you, without her mother, if the marriage was not decided upon. But is that any reason for blighting my hopes? I, also, might say things against you—tell Albert that your friend Puymirol isn't much better than Dargental, and that your intimacy with him has got you into no end of scrapes. But I have no idea of doing so. You have never injured me, why should I try to injure you?"

"So be it," said George, who realised the danger of making an enemy of Mademoiselle Pornic; "I will be silent so far as Albert is concerned, but I must reserve my right to act, as I see fit, with other people."

"In other words, you reserve the right to denounce me if you like. That amounts to the same thing. If I were arrested, even temporarily, Albert would be sure to hear of it. What object can you possibly have in ruining me?"

"None, but I can not allow an innocent person to be condemned. The truth is, my friend Puymirol is accused of the crime, he is under arrest, and I can't abandon him."

"No, certainly not, but it will be easy to prove his innocence, and I will help you. I will testify that he was lunching with us when Dargental was killed. The magistrate is aware of this, however, and I don't see how any suspicion can possibly attach to Puymirol. If there must be a victim, why don't you mention the Countess de Lescombat to the magistrate? She, alone, was interested in having Dargental put out of the way."

These words had scarcely passed Blanche's lips, when her maid entered the room. "Excuse me, madame," she said, "but there is a lady here who insists upon seeing you—the Countess de Lescombat she calls herself."

Blanche and George were both overcome with astonishment. The former hesitated. Her first impulse was to close her doors in the face of the woman whom she so bitterly hated, but she changed her mind. "Show her in," she cried to her maid, who instantly turned to obey the order.

"I had better go," remarked George.

"No, no," replied Blanche. "It is just because you are here that I consent to see her. I want you to hear what she says, for I am satisfied that she has come here about the letters. Go in there, and don't come out until I call you." As she spoke, she pushed George into an adjoining boudoir, the entrance of which was screened by a heavy hanging of silken fabric. George let her do so; the curtain fell; and he considered that he had a perfect right to remain thus concealed, and listen to the conversation which was now about to take place. It was, indeed, needful he should know what part these women had really played in an affair which was costing his friend Puymirol so dear. Presently he heard Blanche ask, in a soft voice: "To what am I indebted for the honour of your visit?"

"Can't you guess?" replied Madame de Lescombat, in a quiet tone, at once steady and well modulated.

"No," replied Blanche, curtly, "though I understand very well that your coming must be due to some pressing need of my assistance."

"I require no one's assistance, I assure you. I have simply an explanation to ask of you."

"It must be of a decidedly dangerous nature, for you to take the trouble to come here in person."

"I am in the habit of attending personally to all matters of a personal nature."

"You are quite right, madame. It is always dangerous to write."

There was a pause, and the two rivals exchanged anything but friendly glances. Blanche had somewhat the advantage, however, for she was at home, and the countess, who had called, must speak the first. "We need not waste any more time on preliminaries," she said, quietly. "I came to speak of Pierre Dargental, I admit it. That man betrayed us both, and he has been justly punished. A man cannot trifle with a woman's honour during years with impunity. Chastisement comes sooner or later. Still, I foresee certain misfortunes which may result from his death."

"I do not understand you," replied Blanche, coldly.

"You think I came here as an enemy." resumed the countess. "What would you say if I told you that Dargental once boasted to me of possessing a letter from you, which he had only to show to have you sent before the assizes?"

"The assizes!" repeated Blanche, scornfully. "Pierre made such a boast as that! If he had sent me there, he would have been obliged to accompany me."

"He is beyond the reach of justice now, for he is dead," replied Madame de Lescombat, "but you are still alive."

"This time, I understand. Why do you use all this circumlocution to tell me that he had the cowardice to show and give you the letter you speak of?"

"And if that were true?"

"I no more fear you than I feared him. He could not denounce me without ruining himself, for what I did was done to save him, and he alone profited by it. With you, madame, the case is very different. If you venture to send my letter to the public prosecutor I shall send him yours."

"Mine!" exclaimed the countess.

"Yes, madame, you cannot have forgotten that you once sent Pierre an impassioned missive in which you spoke of a terrible secret you had confided to him. You placed yourself at his mercy to prove your love."

"And this letter is in your possession?"

"Why shouldn't Pierre have taken the same precautions against you as he took against me? It was not so easy to subjugate me as you, however, for I was in a position to defend myself if he had ventured to attack me."

"I also can defend myself," murmured Madame de Lescombat.

"I hope you will not be reduced to that extremity. Now, let us speak plainly. You did not come here out of kindness of heart to offer to restore me my letter; but I will tell you why you did come. You knew that Pierre had your letter, and you anxiously asked yourself if he might not have entrusted it to me. Well, your ruse has proved successful. You know what to think now. What do you propose?"

"I think we ought to come to an understanding."

"I think so, too," replied Blanche. "We have nothing to gain by war, so let us conclude a treaty of peace. We can exchange letters. Give me mine, and I'll give you yours."

"I haven't yours about me," murmured the countess, visibly embarrassed.

"I am surprised that you left it at home. When a person goes to battle she ought not to forget her weapons."

"I had no idea that our conversation would take such a turn."

"Well, as soon as I saw you come in, I guessed the object of your visit; but, as you are not in a position to carry out your part of the compact, we had better let the subject drop."

"You seem to have no confidence in me. Well, as you refuse to give me my letter until I have returned you yours, why not accompany me home? My carriage is at the door. Take my letter, and come with me. The exchange shall take place in my bedroom. Your letter is locked up in my desk there."

"I am greatly obliged to you for your kind offer, but it is impossible for me to leave the house just now. I am expecting a visit."

"Then name some hour at which it will suit you to come and I will remain at home."

"I shall not be at liberty to-day or to-morrow either, and as your carriage is at the door, it would be better for you to go home and fetch the letter."

"Confess that you refuse to accompany me, merely because you are afraid."

"I do confess it," replied Blanche, calmly. "You have a crowd of servants who would not hesitate to take the letter from me by force if you ordered them to do so. To whom could I complain afterwards? The police would laugh in my face, if I ventured to demand redress. No, I shall not be foolish enough to place myself at your mercy."

"Nor will I place myself at *your* mercy."

"The cases are not the same by any means. This house doesn't belong to me. I am not its only occupant, and my servants are worthy people who would not dare to lay violent hands upon you, a countess. A fine countess, indeed! Octavia Crochard, who used to perform at fairs! Ah! if that were all she ever did! I didn't poison my husband! I did not hire a rascal to murder my lover!"

"What! you have the audacity to accuse me of Dargental's death?"

"I do, and if you persist in holding your head so high, I shall go to the investigating magistrate and tell him so."

"You would make a great mistake, my dear. The murderer has already been discovered—a Monsieur de Puymirol."

"That is absurd! We all know that Puymirol is innocent. The police have made a mistake, that's all; and they would soon realise it if I told the magistrate your story. I should repeat to him the terms of your letter which Pierre showed to me, and which I know by heart. I would even repeat the terms of mine, and confess what I did for Dargental's sake. We should see, then, which of us was in the worst scrape. Take my advice, and don't try and put the blame on Puymirol. He has never been my lover, but he is the intimate friend of my lover's brother-in-law, and if you try to injure him, I swear that you shall repent of it, countess though you are."

George listened to all this with great uneasiness. Madame de Lescombat had just revealed the fact that she was aware of Puymirol's arrest, and that she was inclined to cast upon him the suspicion which she feared might fall upon herself. He was grateful to Blanche for defending Adhémar, and felt a strong desire to interfere, and frighten the countess into strict neutrality. He had the means of doing so in his pocket, as he was the custodian of the letters about which the two rivals were taunting each other. Still he had a lingering fear, that, if he made use of these weapons, they might somehow be turned against Puymirol.

"And now that I see your game," resumed Blanche to the countess, "I shall just prevent it. As soon as you leave the house you mean to go straight to the investigating magistrate and fill his ears with the vilest slander against Puymirol and against me. You shall do nothing of the kind. Before you leave this room you shall write the confession I mean to dictate to you."

"You must be mad!" cried Madame de Lescombat.

"I am nothing of the kind. I am in my own house, and if you refuse to obey me, I shall send word to the commissary of police, and inform him that two old friends of Dargental's have some important revelations to make to him about the murder on the Boulevard Haussmann. He will come and find you here. You may rest assured of that."

"You wretch! do you mean to ruin me?" cried Madame de Lescombat, in consternation.

"Oh! you are not quite so arrogant now. You are afraid of being sent to prison. Ah, well, just state in writing that you came here to entreat me to return you a letter which was written by you to Dargental, and which deeply compromised you."

"No," said the countess, regaining courage. "I will not write a single line. Send for all the commissaries in Paris, and tell them whatever you please. No one will believe you."

"You are very much mistaken. My assertions may not have much weight, but I will produce a witness to support them."

"A witness! what do you mean?" exclaimed Madame de Lescombat, turning perceptibly paler.

Blanche, instead of replying, hastened to the silken curtain, dashed it aside, caught hold of George by the arm, and dragged him into the presence of the now terrified visitor. George was greatly disturbed, for he had not expected this, and did not know what he should say to the countess. He must be careful, at anyrate, for an imprudent word might ruin Puymirol. "Who are you, sir?" asked Madame de Lescombat, when she had partially recovered from her alarm.

"I am Adhémar de Puymirol's most intimate friend, madame."

"Then you are George Caumont. I have often heard you spoken of, but I never supposed that I should find you here, playing the part of a spy."

"I am no spy, madame. It was against my will that I entered that boudoir, and that I listened to your conversation, but now I don't regret having listened."

"You have the courage of your opinions, I see. Well, have the frankness to tell me what use you intend to make of the information you have thus obtained."

"I shall govern my conduct by yours, madame," replied George, looking searchingly at the countess. "If you dare to accuse my friend of a crime he has not committed, I shall accuse you."

"Oh! I merely mentioned that Monsieur de Puymirol had been arrested because I was told so; but as for bothering myself about his affairs, I take no interest in him whatever."

"Then, why did you ask him to go and see you after the show at the Palais de l'Industrie? He went to your house, I know, and until I learn what passed between you two, I have a right to suppose that he has been compromised through your fault."

"Suppose whatever you like, but allow me to leave this house, unless you mean to assist this person in detaining me here by force."

"That is not my intention, but I think she does right to exact guarantee from you."

"I have no idea of writing anything at her dictation, for I scorn her threats, and I defy you to go and tell a magistrate that you listened at the door, or to repeat the conversation you just heard. Assertions are not facts. As for that letter, if it were in mademoiselle's possession, she would have used it against me long ago. If she has it, let her show it. She boasted to several people about having it; but, plainly enough, it was mere brag."

Madame de Lescombat's blow told this time; for Blanche was utterly unable to produce the famous letter. "I boasted about having seen it!" she replied. "Why, where can you have obtained your information? I have never mentioned your letter to anyone excepting Monsieur Caumont, here."

"It was Monsieur de Puymirol who informed me," said the countess.

"Puymirol!" exclaimed George. "That is false!"

"You might be a trifle less rude, sir," responded Madame de Lescombat, coldly. "Your friend came to my house after the horse show. He alluded to his financial worries—which were no news to me, however—and spoke at some length of Pierre Dargental's tragic death. He gave me to understand that I might find myself seriously compromised, but that it was in his power to save me from any serious trouble. I had no fears of that, however, so I declined his offers, but his manner was so strange and his language so embarrassed, that it occurred to me, that he, himself, was afraid of being compromised, and that he was trying to make me share the responsibility of his own conduct. This explains why the news of his arrest did not surprise me very much." George hung his head, for he was afraid that this account of the interview might be true. "This is what I shall tell the magistrate, if he questions me," concluded the countess, with an ironical glance at Blanche. "You, sir, and you, mademoiselle, are at liberty to make use of the weapons you pretend to hold. But your threats don't alarm me, for I know that you have no such weapons at all."

"Are you sure of that?" retorted George. He had already forgotten all his prudent resolutions, and longed to speak his mind freely to this audacious creature. "Your language does not intimidate me, madame," he continued. "You deny that you ever wrote Dargental a letter that might ruin you. Well, I myself have seen that letter, and I am satisfied that if the magistrate saw it, he would immediately issue a warrant for your arrest."

"Was it Monsieur de Puymirol that showed it to you?"

"You have guessed correctly. It was Puymirol. In fact he and I found the pocket-book. Puymirol made a great mistake in trying to profit by one of the lottery tickets it contained, and he has been severely punished for doing so. As for myself, I have made no use of the letters as yet, but I shall, if you force me to do so."

"The letters! There are several, then?"

"There are three."

"Is mine one of them?" asked Blanche, eagerly.

"Yes," was the laconic reply.

"Then, madame here told a falsehood when she said that she had it. I suspected as much," said the actress.

"You also told an untruth," retorted the countess. "And this gentleman doubtless intends to exact hush-money from us."

"I scorn to notice your insults," replied George. "I kept the letters, because I did not know what else to do with them. But now that my friend is compromised, I must take them to the investigating magistrate at once. I shall tell him the whole truth, and though he may blame me, the worst consequences will fall upon the persons who were so deeply interested in regaining possession of their letters. One of them, at least, hasn't shrunk from a crime to recover her property."

"I'm not that one," said Blanche, "and you need no better

proof of that, than my earnest approval of your plan, and my wish that you should see the magistrate as soon as possible."

"Do as you please, sir," said the countess, with pretended indifference. "You mean to try and exculpate Monsieur de Puymirol and to inculpate me. I think, however, that you will only aggravate your friend's situation, for this story of the finding and keeping of the pocket-book does not redound to his credit or to yours. Besides, a magistrate won't accuse a person of my rank merely because a letter of hers is shown to him at the same time as letters from other women of greatly inferior position. If the magistrate suspects any one, it will be mademoiselle here, or else the writer of the third letter; that is, unless the three correspondents are only an invention—I shall only believe your story when I have proof of it."

"I will furnish proof," cried George, yielding to a sudden impulse, and as he spoke he drew the letters from his pocket, and spread them out in his hand in the form of a fan. "Do you recognise yours?" he said to the countess.

Madame de Lescombat turned pale, but made no reply. "I recognise mine," answered Blanche, promptly. "It is the one on the right. Madame's is the one to the left. Dargental once showed it to me, and the handwriting is not of a kind that one is likely to forget."

At this moment the door of the room opened and Albert Verdon swept in like a whirlwind. "George!" he exclaimed, in astonishment. "Well, well, I am delighted to see you! But what the deuce are you doing? Are you playing cards with Blanche?"

At sight of a stranger, the countess lowered her veil, and turned towards the door. As she did so, Albert perceived her, and hastily doffing his hat, stammered: "Excuse me, madame. But I thought Blanche was alone with this gentleman, who is my friend, and who will soon be my brother-in-law."

The countess gave him a keen glance and reflected: "So this young fellow is this girl's lover, and Caumont is about to marry his sister. I am saved. Caumont won't dare to hand the letters to a magistrate." Then, instead of replying to Albert's apology, she bowed to the entire company, and left the room. Blanche responded by a gesture that signified "Good riddance," while George remained so entirely taken by surprise, that he lacked the presence of mind to conceal the letters which the young officer had mistaken for playing-cards. "Well, well," said Albert, "why do you all look so strange? Who was that lady dressed in black? You seemed to be acting a tragedy, together."

"You are about right," said Blanche, gaily. "You have just seen the Countess de Lescombat."

"The lady to whom you wished to send me as envoy extraordinary? And she has paid you a visit? Have you signed a treaty of peace?"

"Oh, no; didn't you notice that she went off in a huff?"

"That's true. She looked furious; but you spoke the other

day of a letter she refused to return to you. Did she bring it back to you to-day?"

"On the contrary, she came to ask me to return a letter of hers. But don't try to solve the mystery. You will not succeed."

"But I must. If you won't tell me anything, I shall apply to George."

"Oh! he's free to tell you what he likes," rejoined Blanche.

George being thus referred to, felt that he could not remain silent, and so, with the best grace he could muster, he began: "You have a right to know the whole truth, my dear Albert. You recollect that I spoke to you yesterday, and again this morning, about my friend Puymirol, and the anxiety his prolonged absence caused me? Well, he has been arrested on the charge of murdering that Monsieur Dargental, who, as you already know, was formerly one of Blanche's admirers."

"Indeed! arrested!" exclaimed Albert. "How can that be? How can suspicion have fallen on him?"

"Listen to me," said George. "I will explain everything;" and thereupon he gave Albert a substantial account of all he knew; the dropping of the pocket-book into the cab; the lunch at the Lion d'Or; the finding of Dargental's dead body; Puymirol's determination to discover the writers of the letters contained in the pocket-book; his subsequent disappearance, his attempt to cash a winning lottery ticket, his arrest, and the search made in the Rue de Medicis. "It was very foolish on Puymirol's part," he added, "for him to conceive the idea of conducting an investigation instead of reporting the facts to the authorities; but it was in vain that I represented to him that he would place himself in a very dangerous position. He first went to the house of the Countess de Lescombat. Ah! I forgot to tell you that one of the letters found in the pocket-book had evidently come from her."

"And was one of the others from Blanche?" asked Albert.

"Yes," replied Mademoiselle Pornic, promptly, "and I will explain it after you have read it. Monsieur Caumont can show it to you."

"Are the letters in your possession?" asked the young officer, looking searchingly at George.

"I have had them for two days past. Puymirol, before calling upon the countess, intrusted them to my keeping, and I have not been able to return them, as I have not seen him since."

"Read my letter," insisted Blanche.

"Are you willing to show it to me?" inquired Albert.

"Perfectly willing," replied George, "and the two others also. Besides, I want your advice in this matter; but it must be given with a full knowledge of all the circumstances. Here are the letters," he added holding them out. "Begin with Mademoiselle Pornic's. The top one won't be interesting to you, as we have no clue to the writer."

"It is very strange," exclaimed the officer, "but I am almost sure that I recognise the handwriting." And at the same time he turned very pale. George looked at him in surprise, and was suddenly seized with the idea that the third missive must have been written by some one closely connected with his future brother-in-law. Accordingly he hastily slipped it between the others, and lowered his hand. He had not been mistaken, for Albert, in a voice husky with emotion, resumed: "I am wrong of course, but give me the letter. I should like to examine it more closely. Why do you hesitate? You must know who wrote it?"

"No! I swear I don't."

"Then show it to me. I have good eyes, and I saw it only too well. I can't remain in this cruel suspense. Give me the letter, I tell you."

George turned pale in his turn. He felt that matters were becoming serious, and he asked himself anxiously how he could get out of the scrape. "My dear Albert," he said, with an evident effort, "you must see that you are placing me in a very embarrassing position. Give me, at least, an explanation that will relieve me of any responsibility. Convince me that you have some serious reason for reading that letter."

"It is so serious that if you refuse to give it me, I will have no further connection with you."

"But whom do you suppose the writer to be?"

"I won't answer you—I can't."

"Then you must excuse me from yielding to a whim which you don't even take the trouble to justify. You threaten to withdraw your friendship, well, I appeal to your reason. If need be, I will leave the matter to umpires of your own selection."

"I cannot explain here."

"That means you distrust me," exclaimed Blanche. "Ah, well, my friend, don't let me stand in your way. I will leave you alone with Monsieur Caumont, and you can talk without fear of being overheard. There is no one in the adjoining boudoir, and I will go to my dressing room, at the other end of the flat."

George and the young lieutenant were left standing face to face, equally agitated and embarrassed. "You promised to show me that letter if I would name the writer," finally said the officer in a hoarse voice.

"But how can you do that? You scarcely saw the letter, and all feminine handwriting is more or less alike."

"This is so familiar, that I cannot possibly be mistaken. It is as well known to me as my sister's."

"Pray don't speak of your sister in connection with this matter," said George entreatingly.

"Would you rather I spoke of my mother?"

"Your mother! What do you mean?"

"She wrote that letter. I am certain of it."

"Impossible! You must be mistaken."

"I should recognise the hand among a thousand."

"You forget that the writer of this missive instigated Dargental's murder," insisted George, imprudently, "for it seems almost certain that she was the guilty party, since it was neither Blanche nor the Countess de Lescombat; and how can you think Madame Verdon capable of such a crime? You never met Dargental. You never even heard of him prior to your arrival in Paris."

"I have not lived with my mother since I was a child."

"But your sister has never left her, and she only heard of Dargental through the papers. Your mother obtained her information about his death from the same source, and it did not affect her in the least."

"How do you know?"

"We at least know that Madame Verdon is preparing for her approaching marriage. Besides, where could she have found a scoundrel willing to risk his life for her sake, in order to kill Dargental?"

"Rochas is capable of any crime," said Albert. George hung his head. He had not been prepared for this reply, and he felt the horror of the situation more keenly than ever. "I am grateful to you for defending her," continued the young officer, gravely, "but I entreat you not to leave me in this cruel uncertainty. Show me the letter."

"If it comes from her, what shall you do?"

"I don't know; but one thing is certain, my sister must know nothing of this."

"You can depend upon my silence. But really I cannot allow you to read the letter."

"So be it," said Albert, with an evident effort. "I shall be satisfied if you will merely show it to me. A single glance will suffice to dispel my doubts. That is enough," he said, bitterly, as George held it out for his inspection, with a trembling hand. "I can no longer doubt."

"Let me burn it here and now," pleaded George.

"Why burn it? On the contrary, you must keep it. It will help you in proving that your friend is innocent."

"Can you suppose I would show it to the investigating magistrate? I bless the chance that brought you here. But for this conversation with you, I should have handed this correspondence to the magistrate in the hope of saving my friend. Now, I would rather die than show him these letters. If you insist upon my keeping them, instead of destroying them, I will submit to your decision; but I fear that they may be taken from me. The search in Puymirol's apartments may be repeated to-morrow, and this time perhaps in my rooms as well."

"You are right; but I am anxious that you should remain armed. Intrust these letters to some one."

"To whom could I safely intrust them?"

"Place them in an envelope, seal it securely, and intrust the packet to a man who would rather let himself be hacked to pieces than give it up, or even open it—in short, give it to Roch Plancoët."

"I scarcely know him."

"But I know him, and I will send him to you."

"I will do as you wish, but—"

"My decision is formed. My mother must leave France immediately, never to return. I will see that she does so, and I will make Gabrielle understand that from this day forth, she and I no longer have a mother. You must devote yourself to your friend. Save him, if you can, and when he is at liberty, advise him, also, to disappear. If he should be obliged to speak of the letters in order to get himself out of the scrape, he can only denounce Blanche and the countess as he does not know the writer of the other letter. If the magistrate questions you, tell him you have burned them all. Now go. I must invent some story to prevent Blanche from guessing the truth. You may expect a visit from me to-morrow morning. I shall have something fresh to tell you then."

George, overcome with emotion, made no response, but staggered out of the house like a drunken man.

## VIII.

Roch Plancoët lived in some modest rooms at the corner of the Rue Royer Collard, but a few steps from the house occupied by Madame Verdon and her daughter. He might have chosen more expensive quarters, for he possessed a small fortune, honestly and laboriously acquired during his long service as superintendent of the Verdon ironworks. But Roch was a philosopher who scorned luxury and adored solitude. He led a quiet life, and he devoted his time and attention almost exclusively to his friends, Gabrielle and Albert—the children of his foster-brother and benefactor. Gabrielle especially was the object of his almost fatherly solicitude. He visited her every day, and her portrait hung in his sitting-room. With her mother, strange to say, he was always very reserved, though he willingly served her when she asked him to do so, which seldom happened, however. The only favour he had ever asked of her, was permission to see her daughter every day, and she had never dared to refuse that, perhaps because she feared him. Roch had held the position of superintendent at the ironworks when she married M. Verdon; and he was too well acquainted with all the incidents of her life, for her to quarrel with him. When she had informed him of her intention to marry M. Rochas, he had replied that she was perfectly free to contract a second marriage if she pleased, and that if she wished to leave her children he would take charge of them. Then, however, had come the announcement of Gabrielle's engagement to George Caumont. George had had the rare good fortune to please Plancoët, and that was a good deal, for the old fellow was very hard to please as far as his favourite's suitors were concerned. However, although Roch had abundant cause for rejoicing at this good news, at least apparently, he returned home thoughtful and preoccupied, and for twenty-four hours merely set foot out of doors to take his meals at a neighbouring restaurant. On the following afternoon, while he was sitting at his window smoking a pipe, Albert Verdon rang at the door. The young officer seemed to be in a state of great excitement, and Roch anxiously asked him: "What is the matter?"

"Ah! my poor friend, you are the only person to whom I can tell the truth," replied Albert. "You know all about my mother's conduct. Well, I have just seen a letter written by her to a lover—"

"To Rochas?" asked Plancoët, eagerly.

"No, no—to that man Dargental whom I spoke to you about, and who was killed in his rooms a fortnight ago." On hearing this Plancoët staggered back to the wall. "Yes," resumed Albert fiercely, "to a scamp who traded on women! A professional black mailer! Ah! the truth is so horrible that on making this discovery I at first thought of flinging myself into the Seine."

"You haven't seen your mother since?" asked Plancoët.

"No, I lacked the courage; I wanted to ask your advice. Come, tell me, did you ever know that my mother carried on an intrigue with that man Dargental?"

"I know all that your mother has done since she became a widow," replied Plancoët, gravely, and then after a little pressing from Albert he proceeded to tell the poor fellow the story of Madame Verdon's profligacy. She had been Dargental's mistress for a time, but he had deserted her for Madame de Lescombat whom he hoped to marry, not, however, without having extorted large sums of money from her, by threatening her with the publication of her correspondence. In fact, only shortly before his death, he had threatened to send her letters to Gabrielle.

Albert was crushed by the sad narrative. At last, however, he mustered strength enough to inform Plancoët of Puymirol's arrest, of the scene at Blanche's house, and the attendant discovery, and of Caumont's present willingness to confide the letters to his keeping. "You must take them," said the young fellow, "and go and see my mother—force her to leave Paris in three days' time, and make her promise to marry M. Rochas abroad, without delay. If she refuses, you may tell her that she will certainly be implicated in the murder of M. Dargental."

"And if she consents?"

"Then you can burn the letters or keep them as you like. But come now, George is waiting for us to hand you the notes."

Roch's face had abruptly assumed an expression of resolution. He did not raise any objection but quietly followed Albert to the Luxembourg Gardens where Caumont indeed was waiting. "My dear fellow," said young Verdon to his future brother-in-law, without more ado, "we are all of the same mind. You know my intentions, and my old friend Roch will see that they are carried out. Will you therefore give him the envelope containing the letters?"

George handed it to Plancoët, who accepted the trust without hesitation. "Are they all here?" he inquired.

"Yes, all three of them," replied the lieutenant. "Break the seal and see for yourself, if you like."

"That is unnecessary; your word is sufficient. But I should be greatly obliged to Monsieur Caumont if he would tell me how his friend Monsieur de Puymirol is getting on."

"His situation remains unchanged. He has been subjected to repeated examinations, but the magistrate has so far come to no decision."

"And your friend has said nothing about the letters?" inquired Plancoët.

"No; and yet, I fancy they would be the only means of saving him."

"Then why doesn't he mention them?"

"Probably because he doesn't wish to compromise the Countess de Lescombat. Perhaps, also, he doesn't want to mix me up in this unfortunate affair. If he spoke of the letters the magistrate would instantly suspect that he had intrusted them to me."

"And do you think that he will remain silent until the end?—that he will let himself be sent before the assizes rather than speak out."

"I feel sure of it. He has many faults, but nothing can subjugate or intimidate him. I know him so well that yesterday I made up my mind to interfere and extricate him from his predicament despite himself; but now I can do nothing for fear of involving Albert's mother in the scandal. He is lost!"

Plancoët, visibly agitated, dropped his eyes. "I feel sure that although Madame Verdon may be very guilty she did not instigate Dargental's murder," he said after a short silence.

"Then who could have instigated it—Rochas?"

"I think not. He would not imperil his life to save a woman's honour. But Albert has told you, I suppose, what he wishes me to do?"

"Yes, sir, and I thoroughly approve of his decision."

"And you are still determined to marry Mademoiselle Verdon?"

"More determined than ever, if she will have me."

"But you are aware that two other persons know that the pocket-book has been found, and are acquainted with the contents of the letters intrusted to you by your friend."

"Blanche Pornic will be silent. I can vouch for her," interrupted the young officer. "And Madame de Lescombat also realizes that it is to her interest to do the same."

"I can proceed to act, then," muttered Plancoët, as if talking to himself.

"I trust you will do so without delay," replied Albert. "My mother is now at home and so is Gabrielle, but you can say that you wish to see my mother alone."

"If you have an opportunity of exchanging a few words in private with Mademoiselle Verdon, pray tell her that my feelings are unchanged," said George to Plancoët.

"I will readily promise you that; and now, as you are acquainted with the habits of the investigating magistrate, will you tell me at what hour I should be likely to find him in his office?"

"Oh! my friend Balmer assured me that he would be in his office all day."

"But why do you wish to know that?" interrupted the lieutenant. "I suppose you have no idea of requesting him to release Puymirol?"

"Certainly not," stammered Plancoët.

"Then hasten to my mother's without delay. Now's your time, but when and where shall we see you again?"

"I am afraid the interview will prove a lengthy one."

"Ah, well, George and I will return here at five o'clock. So good-bye for the present, old friend."

"Farewell," replied Plancoët, pressing the hands the two young men held out to him.

With his head bowed down, the old overseer walked slowly towards Madame Verdon's abode. Gabrielle was upon the balcony, and on seeing him she hastened to the door and let him in. "What is happening?" she asked anxiously. "Just now I received a letter from Albert who tells me he shall come and fetch me at nine o'clock to-night to take me to his colonel's sister, in the Rue de Tournon, for he won't let me stay here any longer."

"Listen, my poor girl," replied Roch, "you must do as your brother asks—besides, it is absolutely necessary, for your mother will leave Paris to-morow."

"To-morrow! but why? That's strange, she surely does not intend to abscond like a criminal?"

"Some transgressions have the same consequence as crimes," said Roch sadly; "believe me—don't try to guess the truth but believe me when I tell you that you must not remain another day under your mother's roof. I swear it by your poor father's memory, by your brother's honour and my own—"

Gabrielle was beginning to understand and tears gathered in her eyes. "Ah!" she murmured in a tone of deep grief.

"But Albert and your future husband will some day tell you more. However, is your mother at home?"

"Yes, in her boudoir."

"Well, I wish to see her and am going there. But before we part let me kiss you and promise me that you will be brave." Then having pressed the poor girl to his heart and imprinted a paternal kiss on her brow he proceeded to Madame Verdon's boudoir.

His interview with the guilty mother was a stormy one—but finally he wrung from her an unwilling compliance with Albert's wishes, and promised her that he would place her letter to Dargental in an envelope and deposit it with his notary, who would hand it to her in exchange for her written consent to Gabrielle's marriage with

George Caumont. Then he hastily left the house, returned home, placed Blanche's and Madame de Lescombat's notes in one envelope addressed to George, and Madame Verdon's in another, and after writing some instructions for his notary, he forthwith repaired to the latter's office. When he left it he paused for an instant, but instead of returning to the Luxembourg to acquaint his young friends with the success of his mission, he finally crossed the Pont St. Michel and proceeded towards the Palais de Justice.

## IX.

WHILE his friend was trying to save him, Adhémar de Puymirol was in a cell at the prefecture dépôt. It was the third day of his imprisonment, and he was pacing, savagely, up and down, like a captive lion in his cage, when suddenly he heard a jailer unbolt the door, and for a moment he deluded himself with the belief that the moment of his release had arrived. All prisoners are subject to these fits of hopefulness. However, this one was of short duration.

"I am ordered to conduct you to the magistrate's office," announced the jailer.

"What for?" replied Puymirol, "I won't answer his questions, so it is not worth while disturbing me."

"It will be the last time. You came here on the 26th. To-day's the 29th, and no one stays here more than three days."

This reply calmed Puymirol. It did not seem to him at all improbable that his case would end favourably, at all events, he would soon know his fate, so he silently followed the warder through the corridors, and up the staircase to M. Robergeot's office. Charles Balmer's friend was still in the prime of life, and had a prepossessing face. He motioned Puymirol to a chair, and the prisoner, as he sat down, curtly exclaimed: "I hope you will put an end to all this, sir."

"It is with that intention that I sent for you," replied the magistrate, "though I might have spared myself the trouble, as you have so far refused to furnish any of the information asked of you; still, I felt it my duty to give you one more chance to tell the truth."

"I have told you all I am going to tell you."

"You have told me nothing. You have even tried to retract the testimony you gave to the commissary of police at the Palais de l'Industrie. You have adopted a most deplorable course. I say nothing about the fact that you presented a lottery ticket that did not belong to you. That is a trifling offence in comparison with the crime of murder, followed by robbery, with which you are charged. It is true I am perfectly satisfied that you did not fire the bullet that killed Dargental, for I admit that an *alibi* has been conclusively established, but this does not prove that you don't know the murderer, and that the crime was not committed in your interest, or in the interest of some person connected with you."

"How can you expect me to prove the injustice of your suspicions? I was well acquainted with Dargental, it is true, but though he may have had enemies, I know nothing about them."

"Well, let me refresh your memory on another point of the case. We have succeeded in finding the cabman who took you to the Lion d'Or, and his testimony proves that you were not alone in his cab in which you claim to have found the lottery tickets. Why did you tell the commissary the contrary?"

"You would have done the same, had you been in my place. I do not wish to subject an innocent person to the same annoyance and discomfort as myself."

"But this person's testimony might be of great service to you. Besides, we shall soon ascertain who your companion was. The cabman already declares that on the day of the murder, and between the hours of half-past eleven and half-past twelve o'clock, he drove two young gentlemen from the Rue de Medicis to the Lion d'Or, and that he had no other fares that morning. He also declares that before leaving the stable that day he had carefully examined the interior of his vehicle, and had not found in it any papers left there by any former passenger. He also declares that nothing extraordinary occurred during the drive referred to."

"We are revolving in the same circle, it seems to me," interrupted Puymirol, "and if you have nothing fresh to tell me—"

"This cabman also declares that a few days after the crime a man who had taken the number of his vehicle came to his residence, which he had ascertained at the company's office, and after giving him twenty francs, questioned him at length about this drive on the 9th of April. The cabman could only tell him what he just told me, viz., that his two passengers alighted at the Lion d'Or in the Rue du Helder. Now, can you tell me why this person inquired after you?"

"No, I can't. Look him up yourself, and ask him the question."

"We *are* looking for him, but though we have not yet succeeded in finding him, I know what he did after his interview with the cabman. I have questioned the employés of the restaurant, among them the door-porter, who tells me that this same man offered him a liberal reward if he would point out either of the two young fellows who breakfasted there in a private room on the morning of April 9th. The porter, who did not know your name, though he knew you very well by sight, promised to do what this person asked, and the latter waited for nearly three weeks, watching for you. You did not show yourself, however, until quite recently; in fact, not until the day previous to your arrest. Then this stranger followed you into the restaurant, and had a long conversation with you, after which you both left the restaurant, though not together. Still, the porter noticed that you followed this stranger up the Boulevard Haussmann. Now, what have you to say to this story? Do you admit that it is true?"

"By no means, but even if I did, what conclusions would

you draw from such an admission on my part?" asked Puymirol.

"That this man was your accomplice; that he was the murderer of Dargental, and that he was trying to communicate with you in reference to a crime which he had committed at your instigation."

"You are going too far, it seems to me. You forget that if this person had acted by my orders he would necessarily have known who I was, and where I lived, and would not have applied to the doorkeeper of a restaurant for information about me."

"You doubtless had your reasons for concealing your name and address. When a man hires a scoundrel to commit a murder, he is usually anxious to keep his identity secret. However, there is a very easy way for you to prove that I am mistaken. That is, to tell me what this man wanted of you, what he said to you at the Lion d'Or, and where you went with him after dinner." This argument was irrefutable, and Puymirol realised it.

"In short," continued the magistrate, "if you will only tell the truth, I can almost promise that you would escape indictment."

Puymirol's eyes flashed. He espied liberty before him—the effacement of his fault, a bright future; but his face suddenly clouded, his features contracted, and he said, with a scornful gesture: "Bah! your clemency could not restore me what I have lost. A man who has spent three days in prison is dishonoured for life. Besides, I haven't a penny, and the only future in store for me is starvation."

"I can prove to you that you have nothing of the kind to fear. You come from Perigord, don't you, and your relatives reside there?"

"My only remaining relative is an aunt who allows me two thousand francs a year; my father left me nothing but debts."

"Which were long since paid by your aunt, Madame Bessèges, who resides at Montpazier, in the department of the Dordogne."

"How do you know that?"

"I have naturally made inquiries about you, and have learned that you belong to an old and highly respected family."

"Oh! We have been ruined for centuries."

"Your aunt made a wealthy marriage, however, and she inherited all her husband's property."

"Yes, but I sha'n't inherit her fortune."

"You have done so already. She died three days ago, after appointing you her sole legatee; and you consequently possess an income of eighty thousand francs. Oh! don't think I am jesting! Since your arrest, all letters addressed to you have been seized at the post-office. This was done by my orders. I hoped that in your correspondence I might find some clue to this mystery, but I was disappointed in that respect. This morning, however, there came a letter from a notary at Montpazier, announcing your aunt's sudden death, and inclosing a certified copy of her will. The document will be given to you as soon as you are set at liberty."

"Then you intend to set me at liberty?"

"That depends entirely upon yourself. The affair of the lottery ticket, and that of the murder, are closely connected, though one is of great, and the other of trifling importance. If you persist in remaining silent, I shall be compelled to believe that you are the culprit, in both cases, for you would not refuse to explain matters if you were merely guilty of a trifling misdemeanour. If you are innocent of the capital charge, you have only to tell me the truth about the finding of the lottery tickets, and I will release you." Puymirol, deeply moved, evidently hesitated. "Pray, recollect," continued the magistrate, "that I shall eventually succeed in solving the mystery without your assistance, so spare me the pain of sending you to Mazas. You are now rich, and public feeling is always very lenient towards the wealthy. Your mishap will soon be forgotten, and your life will become a pleasant one. But, perhaps, you prefer the Assizes? Choose."

Puymirol's choice was already made. Whilst poor, he had been reticent to the verge of heroism. He had not thought it worth his while to purchase freedom by a confession, merely to drag out a miserable existence. He preferred to take his chances of conviction, and profit by his silence afterwards, for he felt sure that the Countess de Lescombat would not fail to reward him eventually. However, he now viewed his situation under an entirely different light. To re-enter the gay world of Paris, which so quickly forgets misdemeanours; to begin life again with plenty of money, that made it well worth his while to yield to the magistrate's entreaties. Besides, as he was well aware, this magistrate already suspected the truth, which truth was likely to come to light at any moment. He had only to question George Caumont, and the latter would probably tell all he knew, reticent as he had been at first. Puymirol reasoned thus, being entirely ignorant of all that had occurred since his arrest. He did not suspect that George was far more deeply interested than himself in concealing the truth about the letters, since one of them, and the only one to which Puymirol attached no importance, had been written by Gabrielle's mother. Being ignorant of this fact, Adhémar naturally supposed that he might venture to confess the truth, without injuring his friend, who felt very little interest in Blanche Pornic, and still less in the Countess de Lescombat. "Well, sir," he began, "I am deeply touched by the kindness and consideration with which you have treated me, and I should be ungrateful, indeed, if I longer resisted your entreaties. I will therefore confess that I know Dargental's murderer."

"At last!" exclaimed M. Robergeot, with a meaning glance at his clerk who had been sitting hard by, idly twirling his pen.

Puymirol then duly acquainted the magistrate with the precise circumstances of the finding of the pocket-book in the cab, on the way to the Lion d'Or, and this point being disposed of he continued: "I am now coming to the most important incident of my story. On the day preceding my arrest, I dined at the Lion d'Or, and had scarcely begun my dinner when I noticed that a gentleman who had taken a seat near me was staring at me with unusual persistency. This gentleman finally seated himself at my table, and then made some very strange disclosures. He began by admitting that he was the person who had thrown the pocket-book into the cab."

"What was his object in telling you that, for he must have had an object in confessing that he had thrown his pocket-book away?"

"He wished me to return it to him."

"Did you comply with his request?"

"No. I replied that I had left it at home, but that I would send it to him if he would give me his address. That he declined to do. He then begged of me to make an appointment to meet him somewhere. I refused, and asked him why he was so anxious to regain possession of an article that was not worth more than fifteen or twenty francs. He made some very poor excuse, and, to try him, I told him I had taken it to the commissary of police in the Chaussée d'Antin, whereupon he seemed greatly disturbed, and after mumbling out some unintelligible excuse, he left me."

"Did you allow the matter to drop there?"

"Wait a moment. I had a plan, and I proceeded to carry it into execution. I had the pocket-book about me at the time, and I have since thought that he must have seen the end of it projecting from my pocket. I did not suspect it then, however, and I took it into my head to find out who he was, for I was as anxious to discover Dargental's murderer as you can be. I thought that by following him at a little distance I should be able to find out where he lived. I adopted this course, and he let me follow him till we reached a lonely spot not far from the Avenue de Villiers; whereupon he turned to the right, into a little street I had never seen before. Here, I unconsciously ventured too near him, for he had concealed himself, and just as I least expected it, he seized me by the throat, throwing me to the ground, and nearly strangling me. When I regained consciousness, I perceived that he had taken the pocket-book from me, and that he was already almost out of sight."

M. Robergeot listened very attentively to this narrative, and when Puymirol paused, he quietly remarked: "The lottery tickets went as well, I suppose?"

"No," murmured Puymirol, slightly embarrassed. "I half suspected that the rascal intended to attack me, so I took the precaution to remove them from the pocket-book. I am sorry now that I did not leave them there, for in that case I should not have been tempted to use them, whereas, if he had yielded to the temptation, you would now have Dargental's real murderer in your power."

"Can you describe this man?" asked M. Robergeot.

"Certainly," replied Puymirol, delighted at this promising beginning. "He was about fifty years of age, and of medium height, though rather strongly built, with a dark complexion, rather keen eyes, and a very energetic face. There was nothing particularly striking about his appearance, but I should recognise him among a thousand."

"Your description agrees with that given by the cabman. But how did this man act when you spoke to him about the murder?"

"I did not speak to him on the subject," answered Puymirol, slightly disconcerted. "The fact is, I was afraid of arousing his suspicions. It was a part of my plan to let him do all the talking. I hoped he would betray himself."

"But you must have asked him why he threw the pocket-book into your cab?"

"Of course, and he replied that there were persons following him, and anxious to rob him, and that he could think of no other way of outwitting them."

"The contents of this pocket-book must have been very valuable, judging by his anxiety to secure possession of it again."

"Perhaps it had contained some bank-notes, but when it came into my hands there was nothing in it but the lottery tickets."

"And it was to recover these lottery tickets that this fellow risked his head?—for he did risk it by entering into conversation with you in a public place, as you had only to denounce him to secure his arrest. In fact, it was your duty to have sent word to a commissary of police while the scoundrel was seated at your table. Come, sir, complete your confession. Confess that there were some letters in the pocket-book—compromising letters, no doubt."

Puymirol turned pale, and hung his head. He saw that he was caught in his own trap. There was no course for him now but to make a clean breast of it. "You are right, sir," he said resolutely, "and I admit that I have done wrong in hiding that fact. There were some letters which I entrusted to my friend, Caumont; but I must add that he consented to accept the trust greatly against his will, and that, from the very first, he urged me to take the pocket-book and its contents to a commissary of police."

"And you say he has these letters?"

"Unless he has burned them, which is not unlikely. He is well acquainted with Balmer, and must have heard of my arrest, so that a fear of injuring me may have led him to destroy the notes."

"It will be very unfortunate for you, and for him, if these letters have disappeared. Did you read them?"

"Yes, and they were all written by women, former sweethearts of Dargental's, evidently. In fact, I feel almost positive that one of these women instigated the murder. However, these letters were none of them signed, so that the best means of getting at the truth would be to find the man who threw the pocket-book into our cab, and who afterwards succeeded in taking it from me. When he is once under arrest, it is probable that he will make a full confession, and name the woman who hired him to commit the crime, for it will be greatly to his interest to throw a part of the responsibility upon her."

M. Robergeot was about to reply, but just then a clerk entered by a side-door, and approaching the magistrate, said a few words to him in a low tone. "Very well, show him in," was the response, and an instant afterwards the door opened for the second time, and George Caumont appeared. His manner was graver than usual; and it was very evident that he was trying hard to repress some strong emotion. He bowed politely to the magistrate, and then walked to Puymirol, with whom he shook hands.

"I am very glad to see you," said Adhémar. "Your testimony will confirm the statements I have just made."

"I will spare you the trouble of questioning this gentleman," interrupted M. Robergeot, and turning to George, he said: "Take a chair."

George silently obeyed, and waited. "Have you brought the letters?" asked the magistrate point blank.

"What letters?" asked George, pretending not to understand.

"The letters that were in the pocket-book."

"I haven't the slightest idea what you mean."

"Oh! your friend here intrusted them to your care."

On hearing this, George, in surprise, glanced at Puymirol, who exclaimed: "You can speak. I have told everything."

Caumont turned pale. He forgot that Puymirol did not know Madame Verdon, so that he could not have mentioned her as one of Dargental's correspondents. "It would ill become me to contradict a man I like and esteem," he said in a voice husky with emotion, "and nothing could have induced me to betray the secret he confided to me, but as he bids me speak, I admit that on the day I saw Monsieur de Puymirol for the last time, he intrusted a package of letters to my care, begging me to take charge of them until his return home. As he failed to make his appearance, I felt very anxious about him. However, Monsieur Balmer informed me that my missing friend was in prison. I also learned from the same source that his rooms had been searched; and as I was perfectly satisfied in my own mind that this search had been made for the express purpose of securing the letters in question, I thought it best to burn them."

"Indeed! Ah! You have done very wrong;" exclaimed the magistrate. "By destroying those letters you have made yourself, in a measure, the accomplice of a murderer."

Here Puymirol, thinking that George was getting them both into trouble, deemed it advisable to interfere. "Confess that you haven't burned them," he interposed, quickly. "You promised to keep them, and your word can be depended upon. You prevaricate from excess of delicacy, and because you are afraid of implicating some of Dargental's old flames. That is absurd. We should be simpletons to compromise ourselves on their account. I would give up the letters, if I had them, without the slightest compunction."

George was suffering terribly. He was on the rack, and his friend seemed to be deserting him. Ah, how glad he would have been to throw the letters on the magistrate's desk, if one of them had not come from Madame Verdon. He now regretted that he had not kept the other two, or, at least, Madame de Lescombat's, for he hated her with all his heart. "I repeat that I have not got them," he said, gloomily.

M. Robergeot was about to put an end to the discussion, when his messenger reappeared, this time with a note which the magistrate tore open carelessly, little suspecting its importance. But he had scarcely glanced at it, when his expression changed. "Who gave you this letter?" he inquired, eagerly.

"A man who is waiting for an answer."

"Very well; go and tell him that I will ring for him in a few moments. Until then, don't lose sight of him, and if he attempts to go away, detain him, by force if necessary, even if you have to call upon the guards for assistance." As soon as the messenger had left the room, M. Robergeot turned to the two young fellows and said: "To which of you am I indebted for this mystification? For it is the work of one of you, I feel certain." Then, seeing them look at each other in very natural astonishment: "These are the terms of the letter I have just received," he continued. "'Pierre Dargental's murderer desires an immediate interview with the magistrate. He gives himself up, but he has some revelations to make before the magistrate signs the order for his detention.' Now, have you any knowledge of this strange culprit? Am I indebted to you for bringing him to light?"

"What possible motive could we have had?" asked George.

"Then you have no idea who he is?"

"Not the slightest."

"Well, I am now about to send for this man," resumed M. Robergeot, gravely. "Remain seated, and say nothing, whoever he may prove to be. You must not speak till I have finished."

"Very well," replied Puymirol; "but you won't forbid me to look at him, and if it is my acquaintance of the restaurant, I will warn you by a sign. If I recognise him, I will raise my hand to my forehead."

"So be it; but confine yourself to that. As for you, Monsieur Caumont, I give you permission to do the same, if you recognise this man as the person who threw the pocket-book into your cab on the Place du Carrousel."

George remained silent. He had not yet admitted that he was in the cab at the time, and he did not deem it advisable to admit it now. M. Robergeot did not insist, however. He rang, and the stranger entered, closely followed by the messenger, and advanced towards the desk at which the magistrate was seated; but on perceiving the two friends, whom he had failed to notice at first, he turned pale, and stopped short. Puymirol found it very difficult to keep quiet, for he had recognised the mysterious stranger of the Lion d'Or at the very first glance. He restrained himself, however, and, without a word, passed his hand across his forehead. George Caumont, on his side, remained silent and motionless; but every vestige of colour had fled from his cheeks, leaving him even paler than the visitor who declared himself to be Dargental's murderer. "Come, sir," the magistrate said to the new comer, without inviting him to be seated, "I do not suppose that you came here to play a joke on me; but I can not help wondering if you are in your right mind. I warn you that I have no time to lose. So explain the meaning of the extraordinary letter I have just received from you. I should mention that these gentlemen are suspected of being accomplices in the crime of which you accuse yourself. I, therefore, that they should hear what you have to say."

"They accomplices!" exclaimed the stranger. "I declare that they are both innocent. I had no accomplices."

"Then you don't know either of these gentlemen?"

However, instead of falling into the trap set for him, the new comer coolly replied: "I don't know their names, but I have seen them before. I have even had a long conversation with one of them. That one," he added, pointing to Puymirol.

"Where, and under what circumstances?"

"At the restaurant known as the Lion d'Or, which I entered for the express purpose of speaking to him."

"That is perfectly true!" cried Puymirol, delighted to hear the culprit confirm the testimony he had given.

"And where did you see that gentleman?" asked the magistrate, pointing to George Caumont.

"I saw him but once in a cab on the Place du Carrousel."

"Well, why was it that you killed Pierre Dargental, on the 9th of April last?"

"Because he refused to surrender to me some letters which he intended to use against a woman."

"But why did you interest yourself in her behalf?"

"I was in love with her. She is a married woman, and Dargental threatened to denounce her to her husband, who would have killed her, had he seen those proofs of her infatuation."

"So you became a murderer through love and devotion?" said M. Robergeot, ironically. "We will see by-and-by how the jury appreciate these extenuating circumstances. In the meantime, if you wish me to believe you, you must give me the name of this woman who was, of course, your accomplice."

"No, sir; I acted entirely without her knowledge or consent. She is absolutely ignorant of what I have done."

"Then you refuse to give me her name?"

"Is it likely that I have risked my life, and surrender it to you, in view of betraying the woman I have sworn to save? Take my life; it is yours; but I shall carry my secret with me to the grave."

George's face brightened, and Puymirol could not help showing his admiration for this heroism on the part of the man he had so bitterly anathematized. "You fancy that this secret will die with you," replied the magistrate; "but I think I shall succeed in discovering it. I believe I am already on the track." And then, gazing searchingly at the stranger, M. Robergeot said;

"We will return to this subject presently. You must now give me the particulars of the murder."

"It is for that purpose that I came here," replied the new comer, coldly. "I called on Dargental at about eleven o'clock, on the morning of April 9th. He admitted me himself, ushered me into the dining-room, and left me in order to enter his bed-chamber. He returned a moment afterwards with a pistol in his hand; and I had scarcely begun to explain the object of my visit, before he began to abuse me in the most insulting manner. He showered offensive epithets upon me, and uttered the most violent threats against the person whom I wished to place beyond the reach of his knavery. He declared that if she did not pay him the sum of two hundred thousand francs before two days had expired, he would send the letters she had been so imprudent as to write him, to her husband. He added that these letters were then in his pocket, ready to be produced at any moment. Frantic with rage, I sprang at his throat. He freed himself, and threatened me with his pistol; I tried to wrest it from him, but during the struggle, and at a moment when the barrel of the pistol was pointed at his breast, the weapon went off."

"And the bullet pierced Dargental's heart? This was a most unlucky chance. You are remarkably clever. You almost convince me that you were acting only in self-defence, and that the crime you committed was simply justifiable homicide. Well, what after?"

"I lifted the body, placed it in an arm-chair, searched all his pockets, found the note-case he always carried upon his person, opened it, satisfied myself that the letters were there, placed it in my pocket, and left the house without even taking the precaution to wash my blood-stained hands."

"Which left stains upon the lottery tickets you had handled?"

"That is true; I recollect now, that there were some lottery tickets in one of the compartments of the pocket-book."

"Well, you have not told me all. What occurred afterwards?"

"I left the house, fully intending to return home and burn the letters, after showing them to the writer, but, on the Boulevard Haussmann, I saw two men who pretended to be strolling along, looking into the shop windows, but whom I instantly recognised, in spite of their disguise, as two men of a detective agency, whom the lady's husband had hired to watch his wife. Dargental had sent him anonymous letters about her and me. They started after me, and at the corner of the Rue de Rivoli and the Rue des Pyramides one of them stopped to speak to a policeman, while the other continued to follow me. I watched the movements of the policeman out of the corner of my eye, and saw that he refused to interfere. The next one we met might prove less scrupulous, and I might be arrested and taken to the station-house, where I should certainly be searched, and the letters found upon me. I realized my danger, and felt that I had not a moment to lose in getting rid of the letters, so without stopping to reflect, I adopted the first plan that occurred to me. I was just passing one of the outlets of the Place du Carrousel. There was a long line of vehicles. The private detectives were following me at a little distance, talking together, probably making arrangements to pick a quarrel with me, in order to attract the attention of the police, who would take us to the station house. At all events their conversation was so animated that they forgot to watch my movements. In the last cab on the line I saw two gentlemen. The window was open, and I dropped the pocket-book inside, carefully noting the number of the vehicle as I did so. The two detectives gave me no further trouble, however, as no policeman would consent to lend them a helping hand, still they followed me to Montrouge. There is a house there with which I am familiar, and which has two outsets. I entered it, and made my escape by one door, while the two rascals were talking with the porter at the other."

"Is this all you have to tell me?" inquired M. Robergeot.

"Yes, sir," the man replied, coldly. "You now merely have to send me to prison."

"Which I shall proceed to do so as soon as certain formalities are complied with. Your disclosures were so unexpected that I quite forgot to ask your name, profession, age and residence."

"It is useless to ask me for information that I can not give."

"And why not?"

"Because I should betray a secret that is not my own. If I told you who I am, you would soon know the woman I wish to save."

"You hope to die like Campi, who was executed without any one having been able to discover his real name. Your case does not resemble his in the least, however."

"No, certainly not, and I shall die in an entirely different way, but I shall die unknown."

This was said in a tone that made M. Robergeot wonder if he were not dealing with a madman. "But your deposition must be signed," said he.

"Oh! I am quite ready to acknowledge in writing that I have told the truth, and that I have nothing to retract, but I shall sign the first name that occurs to me."

The magistrate felt that it was time to put an end to this discussion. He knew that time and solitude overcome the most stubborn resistance; besides, the presence of the two friends was a constraint upon him. "So be it," said he. "I shall question you again, however, after you have had time for reflection. In the meantime, you can write your acknowledgment, after first reading the deposition you have just made."

The stranger thereupon rose up, approached the clerk's table, took a pen, and then at the bottom of the last page of the report of his evidence he wrote these words: "I declare that I persist in my statements correctly recorded above: that I alone, and of my own free will, killed Pierre Dargental; that no one prompted me to commit the crime, and that no one knew I was the perpetrator of the murder, until I made the above confession in the presence of Monsieur Robergeot, and of two gentlemen unknown to me."

He then handed the document to the magistrate, who, after glancing at it, said quietly: "Very well. You will now be taken to the dépôt."

But all at once the man retreated to the wall, which was only three or four steps from him, put his hand in his overcoat pocket, and drew out a weapon that elicited an exclamation of dismay from the magistrate. This weapon was one of those old-fashioned horse pistols, rarely seen now-a-days, and before any one could reach the stranger, he had raised this fire-arm to his head and pulled the trigger. A loud explosion shook the walls; a cloud of smoke filled the office, and drops of warm blood spurted in Puymirol's face. The murderer was lying motionless at the foot of the wall—dead. The witnesses of this sudden suicide stood for a moment overcome with horror. The guard, who had escorted Puymirol into the room, looked as white as a sheet, though he was an old soldier. The clerk, in his alarm, had entered the office without waiting for M. Robergeot to ring. "Fetch the commissary of police on duty here in the palace," said the magistrate. "I, myself, will summon the public prosecutor. Your examination is ended for the present, gentlemen. You, Monsieur Caumont, are at liberty to retire, but you must hold yourself in readiness to appear before me at any moment, for this affair is not ended. You, Monsieur de Puymirol, will return to the dépôt, and remain there until I send for you which will be in a short time, probably."

George rushed wildly through the passages, and it was not until he found himself out of doors that he again breathed freely Where could he find Albert? They had parted in the Rue de Medicis, after vainly waiting for Roch Plancoët to join them in the garden of the Luxembourg. George had, of course, been obliged to follow the messenger sent to conduct him before the magistrate; and Albert had parted from him with a cheery: "I'll see you again to-morrow." But George now wanted to see the young officer at once; for the man who had just blown his brains out in the presence of the two friends was Roch Plancoët, and it had cost George no little effort to conceal his emotion on seeing him enter M. Robergeot's office. Why had he killed himself? and why had he declared to George's profound astonishment that he was Dargental's murderer? Evidently to spare Gabrielle the pain of knowing her mother's disgrace. But what a strange means he had employed! Could he have really believed that the authorities would always remain ignorant of his name? He had certainly disfigured himself beyond power of recognition, but justice possesses other means of establishing a person's identity. Besides, was his statement really correct? The story of the agents despatched to watch him by M. Rochas was very extraordinary, and yet, otherwise, why had he thrown the pocket-book into the cab?

Whilst thus reflecting, George Caumont reached the Place Saint-Michel. Some omnibuses there barred his passage, and while waiting to pass, he saw Madame Verdon approaching him. He tried to avoid her, but it was too late. She called to him, and said: "Well, are you satisfied? You have leagued yourself with Albert and Gabrielle, I see, so as to force me to leave Paris, and you have even sent Monsieur Plancoët to me with your orders. You deserve to marry a girl who rebels against her mother. However, farewell, and good luck to you," she added, with a sneering laugh. "I have just been to Plancoët's notary and have left him my written consent to your marriage. Monsieur Rochas is waiting for me, and I must make haste if I want to catch the express for Rome, *via* Florence."

With these concluding words, she entered a passing cab, leaving George amazed and indignant beyond expression. On his way up the Boulevard Saint-Michel he was obliged to pass Madame Verdon's residence, and he felt strongly tempted to enter it. Gabrielle was there, no doubt, but what should he say to her? How could he explain to her, her mother's conduct, and acquaint her with the tragical death of her old friend, Roch? It would certainly be better to allow her brother time to prepare her for this blow. Accordingly he walked straight on to the Rue de Medicis. Here his doorkeeper handed him a note from Albert which ran as follows: "Everything has been arranged. I have seen my sister, and this evening I shall take her to the house of Madame de Brangue, my colonel's wife, who will act as her chaperon for the present. Call on me to-morrow morning, at nine o'clock, at the Hôtel de l'Empereur Joseph, in the Rue de Tournon. Try to find Plancoët before you come, and bring him with you. His visit to my mother accomplished wonders. What a friend we have in him! He has saved us all."

"At the cost of his life!" murmured George, sorrowfully, for he did not share the illusions of his future brother-in-law.

However, he was punctual in keeping the appointment that Albert had made with him for the following morning, and on reaching the hotel he found the lieutenant smoking a cigar in his room. The first words that the young officer articulated were: "Where is Plancoët? Didn't you bring him with you?"

George shook his head. He did not know how to break the terrible news to his prospective brother-in-law. "Plancoët will never come," he at last said, sadly.

"Why? has any accident happened to him?"

George was about to reply that he was dead, when one of the hotel servants entered with a letter which he handed to Albert. "Why, this note is from Roch," exclaimed the young officer in astonishment. "How strange for him to write instead of coming to see me. The letter must have been posted yesterday evening. Let us see what he has to say."

He broke the seal, and drew from the envelope two sheets of paper which George had only to glance at, to recognise the letters of Blanche Pornic and the countess. Albert laid them on the table and then opening the missive from Plancoët which accompanied them, he read aloud as follows: "'My dear boy,—You, as yet, only know a part of the truth, and you must know it all. You will henceforth be the head of the family; and until your sister marries, you will be responsible for her, for I shall not be at hand to watch over her.'"

"Why, what can he be driving at?" exclaimed the lieutenant. "Roch is the best fellow in the world, but he has a fondness for making a mystery out of everything.

"'I am sure that your mother will yield,'" he continued, resuming his perusal, "'and it is hardly probable that you will ever see her again. That is why, before I go to see her, I wish to make you clearly understand the part she has played in an affair which has proved so terrible in its consequences to us all, and to me especially. I need not revert to the past, nor need I speak of your mother's fault. I can only plead extenuating circumstances on her behalf. While your poor father lived she did not fail in her duty. She brought you up carefully, your sister and yourself; she even loved you devotedly. It was her husband's death that caused all this misery. Left to herself, and transplanted to Paris, she lacked the strength to resist the many temptations of her new life; and fate willed that she should meet a scoundrel who only thought of profiting by her weakness. He wanted to marry her for her money, but I managed to prevent that, though she fell a willing victim to his fascinations. She finally discovered, however, that she had several rivals in his affections, and a rupture followed. She could not escape from Dargental's persecutions; his demands never ceased, and latterly, they assumed such a threatening character that I resolved to put an end to them. I could not choose my means in doing this. It was absolutely necessary to secure the restitution of a letter which Dargental had threatened to send to Monsieur Rochas, in case your mother did not consent to purchase it at a cost of two hundred thousand francs; and I could not hope to obtain it from Dargental by persuasion. Your mother was terribly frightened, and wished to marry as soon as possible in order to have a protector capable of defending her. I took good care not to say a word to her about the plan which I had formed, and which I executed without anybody's help. I resolved to kill Dargental, and I did kill him!'

"Plancoët a murderer! impossible!" exclaimed the lieutenant.

"I knew it," murmured George. "Go on to the end, my friend."

Albert was in consternation, but he, nevertheless, continued: "'I killed him, after a violent altercation which would almost justify me in pleading that I only acted in self-defence; but I believe I should have killed him in any case. This man would have cast a shadow over Gabrielle's whole life. He was a disgrace to mankind. I secured the letter which he had intended to use as a weapon against your mother and yourselves, and I left the house;

and we should have all been saved but for a strange fatality. When you see Monsieur Caumont again, ask him to explain how he and his friend, Monsieur de Puymirol, came into possession of the pocket-book I had taken from Dargental, and tell him that I was the person who threw that pocket-book into their cab. He will guess the rest, and explain everything to you. I enclose in this note the letters written by the two ladies I do not know. I keep the third, which will be useful to me in negotiating with your mother. If she accepts the conditions we have agreed to impose upon her—as I have no doubt she will—I shall leave her letter with Monsieur Berlier, my notary, who resides at No. 7 on the Quai Saint-Michel, with instructions to give it to your mother in exchange for her written consent to your sister's marriage with Monsieur Caumont.'"

"The exchange has been effected," said George. "I met your mother as she was leaving the notary's office."

"'And this is what I have resolved to do, whatever the result may be:'" resumed Albert, still reading Plancoët's letter: "'Monsieur Caumont's most intimate friend has been arrested, and is still in prison, charged with a crime of which he is innocent. He shall not remain there any longer. I will not permit it. I shall call upon the magistrate this very day, and inform him that it was I who killed Dargental. He will ask me why I killed him, and I shall be obliged to invent some story that will screen your mother from suspicion. He will also ask my name; but I shall refuse to give it, and I shall kill myself in the magistrate's presence.'"

"He must have been crazy when he wrote that," said Albert.

"He did kill himself, I saw him do so," rejoined George.

"Good heavens! is it true? you were present at the time?"

"Yes," said Caumont; and he forthwith related all that had taken place in the magistrate's office.

"Poor Roch!" murmured the lieutenant, dashing away a tear. "He sacrificed his life for our sake, I see that. But I have not finished his letter; let me read on to the end: 'I mean to shoot myself in such a way that I shall be absolutely disfigured. There are no marks on my linen, no tailor's name on my clothes; I have even pulled the lining out of my hat so that my identity will always remain a mystery for the officials. My notary will hand you a power of attorney enabling you to attend to my affairs, for I have told him and the doorkeeper at my house that I am going to America. Nobody will pay any attention to my disappearance. Believe me when I say that your mother is quite guiltless in all this. Puymirol also; Rochas, too, knew nothing about it, though Dargental had sent him anonymous letters, and he was having me watched, believing me to be your mother's lover. Dargental would have brought disgrace upon you all. He would not have stopped at anything: he was so very furious that he could not obtain a large sum of money from your mother. There was but one course to follow—to put him out of the way—and I adopted it. And now, God bless you! Think of me sometimes. Give Caumont Gabrielle's portrait which hangs in my sitting-room. Good-bye, my dear Albert, my last thought will be for you all.'"

A spell of silence followed this perusal. There were tears in the young men's eyes. However, finally, Caumont remarked: "It seems as though Roch's suicide will really end the investigation. His body will not be identified, and the affair will be forgotten, providing we prevent any imprudent act calculated to revive it."

"An imprudent act! We shall certainly not commit any."

"No; but we can't foresee what the writers of those letters will do. Even now, they may be shuddering at the thought of being compromised; and fear is a bad adviser."

"You are right, and I think it would be as well to return the letters to them immediately—the sooner the better. Let us take a cab, and call on them."

Caumont assented; and five minutes later, he and Albert were rolling through the streets of Paris, bound first for Blanche's rooms in the Avenue de Messine, and thence for the Lescombat mansion near the Parc Monceau.

. . . . . . . . .

But little more now remains to be told; Blanche received her letter, and the countess received hers; and both missives were duly burnt without delay. Three weeks after Roch Plancoët's death, George and Gabrielle were married at the church of St. Sulpice. The bride was, perhaps, a trifle sad as her brother and her happy spouse had been obliged to inform her of Roch's suicide, and even amid her bliss, she could not entirely forget the worthy old friend, who had sacrificed himself for her and hers. M. Robergeot had failed to penetrate the identity of Dargental's murderer, so thorough had been the precautions which Roch had taken; and to the authorities, if not to our readers, the crime of the Boulevard Haussmann still remains a puzzling mystery.

Madame Verdon is now married. She was united at Florence to M. Rochas, who rules her with an iron hand. Puymirol, having been duly released, has converted his Aunt Bessèges's property into cash and left for New York, where he hopes to find a rich wife, but the Americans are shrewd, and his sanguine expectations may not be realised. Poor Charles Balmer is furious. A celebrated physician has just informed him that he has thirty more years to live, and he has only money enough left to last him eighteen months. Albert is fast becoming an able officer, and is daily expecting promotion; while as for George and Gabrielle they are really happy, and still remember Roch Plancoët, who died to insure them a peaceful, unclouded life.

THE END.